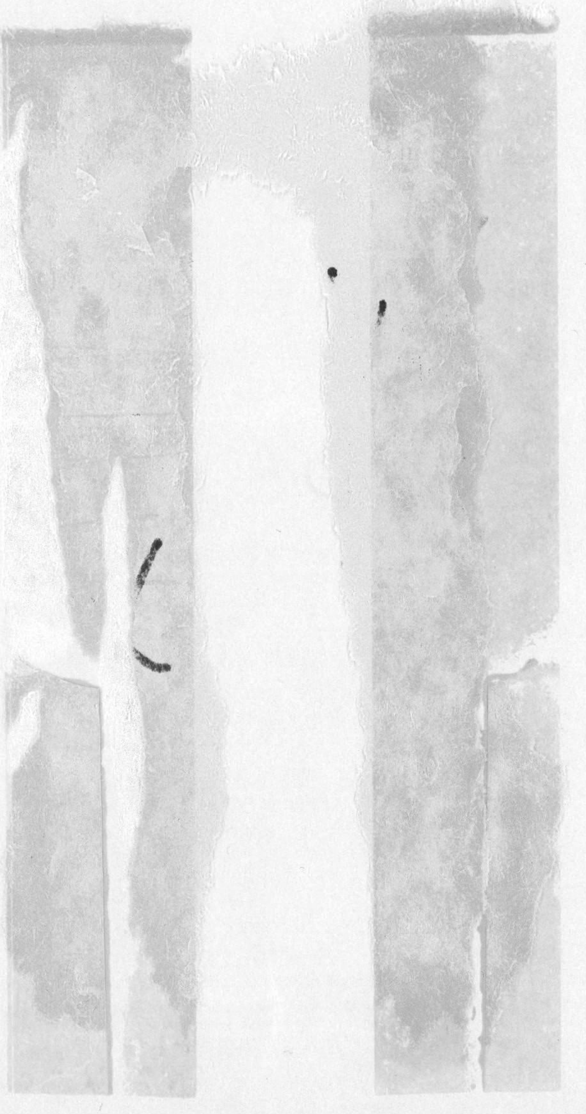

DANCING·IN ·THE·DARK·

The Toby Peters Mysteries

BULLET FOR A STAR
MURDER ON THE YELLOW BRICK ROAD
YOU BET YOUR LIFE
THE HOWARD HUGHES AFFAIR
NEVER CROSS A VAMPIRE
HIGH MIDNIGHT
CATCH A FALLING CLOWN
HE DONE HER WRONG
THE FALA FACTOR
DOWN FOR THE COUNT
THE MAN WHO SHOT LEWIS VANCE
SMART MOVES
THINK FAST, MR. PETERS
BURIED CAESARS
POOR BUTTERFLY
THE MELTING CLOCK
THE DEVIL MET A LADY
TOMORROW IS ANOTHER DAY
DANCING IN THE DARK

DANCING IN THE DARK

STUART M. KAMINSKY

THE MYSTERIOUS PRESS

Published by Warner Books

A Time Warner Company

Mysterious Press books are published by Warner Books, Inc.,
1271 Avenue of the Americas, New York, NY 10020.

A Time Warner Company

Printed in the United States of America

First printing: January 1996

10 9 8 7 6 5 4 3 2 1

Library of Congress Cataloging-in-Publication Data

Kaminsky, Stuart M.
Dancing in the dark / Stuart M. Kaminsky.
p. cm.
ISBN 0-89296-528-2 (hc)
1. Peters, Toby (Fictitious character)—Fiction. 2. Motion picture actors and actresses—California—Los Angeles—Fiction. 3. Private investigators—California—Los Angeles—Fiction. 4. Los Angeles (Calif.)—Fiction. 5. Astaire, Fred—Fiction. I. Title.
PS3561.A43D36 1996
813'.54—dc20 95-13095
CIP

This one is for Henry Kraus, who had faith and a smile and taught me to dance. If he could teach me, he could teach Helen Keller.

Good Lord I thought I was prepared
but I wasn't prepared for that.
—Bert Williams

DANCING IN THE DARK

Chapter One

Black Bottom

"First you put your two knees close up tight," I said, my hands behind my back, nodding in approval as she followed my instructions.

"Now," I went on, "you swing them to the left, then you swing them to the right."

She started the first swing left, stopped, and eyed me skeptically.

We were in the middle of the dance floor of the Monticello Hotel on Sunset which, until a few years ago, had been the St. Lawrence Hotel. All the chairs had been pushed back to give us room and the word had gone out to the staff that Miss Luna Martin and I were to be left alone, except for the ancient piano player who sat at his instrument on a slightly raised bandstand, waiting for me to give him orders.

"You sure this is the tango?" she said, her hands on her hips.

Luna Martin had short, very blond and curly hair, a pale round face, and large, very red lips. She had a few extra pounds in her hips but she looked good in her white silk blouse and tan slacks. And she was ready to learn the tango. From me.

I was pushing fifty, had the battered face of a washed-up

middleweight, and didn't know a tango from a funeral march. But if I didn't convince the lady I could teach her to dance, my client was on the verge of having his nimble feet dipped in concrete, after his toenails were trimmed down to the knuckles.

"Well," Luna said, tapping her foot, "I am waiting."

Luna, I had noticed, used no contractions. She also used no control over her patience. She didn't have to. She was the girlfriend of Arthur Forbes, formerly known as Fingers Intaglia for having indelicately removed the fingers of people who annoyed him or his pals in the Purple Gang. Arthur Forbes was well-known in Los Angeles in 1943. He owned four downtown office buildings, a contracting company, a chain of hardware stores, and the hotel in whose ballroom I now stood, not knowing what the hell I was doing.

My name is Toby Peters. I'm a private investigator. *Investigator* sounds better than *detective*. *Detective* sounds like comic strips and radio shows, Dick Tracy and Sam Spade and Johnny Dollar. *Investigator* isn't quite class, but it doesn't send you into the game with a handicap. I sell my battered face and a reputation for dogged determination, loyalty to clients, and knowing how to keep my mouth shut. I could not live by my dance skills, though there now seemed to be the possibility that I might die by my ignorance of the tango.

"It's the Gazpacho Tango. The latest thing from Argentina. I think the problem is we need music. Take a short break and I'll tell Lou what to play."

Luna Martin did not look convinced. She had reason to not look convinced.

"Two minutes," she said, pointing a long and threatening red fingernail in my direction.

"Two minutes," I agreed with my most winning smile,

which, I have been told, makes me look like a constipated water buffalo.

She moved to a nearby table where she had piled everything you need for a dance lesson—a pitcher of ice water with two glasses, a Monticello Hotel towel neatly folded, a pair of glistening black tap shoes, and a sweater.

I moved to the bandstand and took the three steps up to Lou Canton who sat at the piano bench, a copy of the March *Woman's Day* propped above the keys where sheet music was supposed to sit.

"She wants to tango," I whispered.

"So," he said with a shrug, "I play a tango. But you ask me, send her to Arthur Murray's. They've got a dollar-fifty-a-week special offer going."

Lou was eighty years old, the regular piano player at the Mozambique Lounge in Glendale. I'd met him a couple of weeks earlier on a case. Lou was a stringy guy with a bad dye job on his hair and mustache. He looked a little like Clifton Webb probably would in thirty years. Lou's philosophy was simple: Make a buck if you can and say whatever you feel like saying because when you're eighty what're they going to do to you? I could tell Lou what Fingers Intaglia was capable of doing.

"Astaire taught me the fox-trot and the waltz," I said, ignoring Lou's advice. "She doesn't want to fox-trot. She doesn't want to waltz. She wants to tango. How do you tango?"

Lou looked up at me and shrugged his bony shoulders. His red suspenders tightened and so did his lips. I looked across the room at Luna, who put down her glass of water and looked at her gaudy gold wristwatch.

"I don't know from tango. Fake it," Lou said.

"Fake it? You played with Isham Jones, Paul Whiteman, Claude Thornhill, and you don't know how to tango?"

"I know how to *play* tangos," he said. "Who looks close at the feet?"

"Any suggestions?"

"Tap," he said. "Easier to fake. I play something bouncy and you fake it. Like Cagney. I played a couple of times for Cagney. He made it up as he went along. Lots of confidence. A good smile and moving all over the place."

"That's it?"

"All I can give you," he said. "That and a two-cent *Woman's Day* that was sitting here."

He handed me the magazine. I folded it and stuck it in my back pocket. Luna was back in the middle of the dance floor. My two minutes were up.

"Play fast and loud," I whispered, patting the piano and heading back to my student. "Put on the tap shoes," I said brightly.

"I want the tango," she said. "Arthur wants me to learn the tango. None of us wants to disappoint Arthur. Not you. Not me. Not ever."

"Mr. Astaire specifically said that before he gives you the next lesson, I should teach you a short tap routine he showed me," I improvised. "He wants to dance it with you."

"Really?" she said, showing impossibly perfect white teeth.

"Would I lie to a friend of Mr. Forbes?"

"It would be unwise," she said and headed for her tap shoes. I turned to Lou for long-distance suggestions. He had none, but his fingers began to hit the keys. He played "Nola" as loud as the Steinway would let him. It didn't sound bad except for a single clinker of a piano key.

Luna got her tap shoes on and came clicking back to me.

"I'm not enamored of that song," she said. "Arthur once had a friend named Lola."

"The song is 'Nola,'" I said.

"That's close enough," she said.

"Gotcha," I said and turned to shout, "Lou, how about a different song?"

"One that's not named for a girl," Luna said.

"One that's not named for a girl," I shouted to Lou.

Lou stopped playing for a second, shook his head, and clearly said, "*Meshuganah.*"

He launched into "I've Got a Gal in Kalamazoo," which I thought was pushing things a little, but Luna nodded her approval. Lou hit the bad note again and rushed on past it.

"Okay," I said over the music. "You pick up the beat and do a left-foot double heel and toe followed by a right-foot heel and toe and then a shuffle and a turn. Got that?"

I didn't know what the hell I was talking about, but Luna nodded with a slightly puzzled look on her determined, pretty face and said, "I think so. Show me."

"Didn't bring my tap shoes," I said apologetically. "Wore right through the taps. They're being resoled at a place over on . . ."

"Show me," she said with a smile I did not like.

It was my turn to nod. My first problem was that I couldn't find the beat, though I heard Lou hitting it hard. Something is wrong with the spring inside me. By the time I hear the beat, it's long gone. My former wife, Anne, tried to teach me to dance at least once a year and gave up each time in quiet cold disbelief, certain that I wasn't trying hard enough. Even Fred Astaire hadn't been able to get through to me.

I did my best to imagine I was Astaire, put on a happy face, and tried to remember what I had just told Luna. I plunged in. Heel-toe, heel-toe, arms out, happy smile, shuffle and turn. I almost fell on the turn but I converted it to a bow in Luna's general direction. She had just witnessed the march of the wooden klutz.

"I think I got it," she said seriously.

"Fine," I said. "Give it a try."

"Can we restart the music? I am not so good at picking up the beat."

"Lou," I called. "Take it from the top."

Lou stopped, muttered something, and was off to Kalamazoo. Luna started in, taps clicking. She had feet of solid lead and the grace of an armadillo. She was Ruby Keeler coming out of a heavy dose of ether. She tapped, she shuffled, she stopped and looked to me for approval. It was hard to believe that she had actually given dance lessons to sane people, but that's what she had claimed.

"Almost perfect. Only the reverse. Start with the left foot," I said.

She did. Over and over again. Lou switched to "The Mexican Hat Dance." The move in no way altered Luna Martin's style or pace.

I looked on critically, hands behind my back, watching the clock for the hour to end. I gave her a break, let her use the ladies room, the towel, and the pitcher of water.

Lou lifted the top of the piano and grumbled as he searched for the bad note.

"Wire's about to go. No middle C," he grumbled.

"Do without it," I said.

Luna announced that she was, again, "Ready."

Lou closed the top of the piano.

And then, back to the routine.

I'll give her this. She was determined. The hour sulked by to the uneven tapping of dancing feet and the piano magic of Lou Canton, who played loudly and with no enthusiasm "Where Oh Where Has My Little Dog Gone" and "After You've Gone." There was a tense moment when Lou banged into "Ida! Sweet As Apple Cider." Luna stopped in the middle of a shuffle and said, "That is a girl's name."

"Forbes had a friend named Ida?" I asked.

"It is the principle of the thing, Mr. Peters," she said with indignation.

"Lou," I shouted. "You're playing a girl's name."

He stopped and shouted sarcastically, "I'm sorry. I don't know how I could make such a mistake. I'll cut off my fingers."

Don't give the lady any ideas, I thought, and was about to make a suggestion when he roared into "If I Could Be with You One Hour Tonight."

"You crazy old nut," Luna shouted.

Lou ignored her.

According to the big Benrus clock on the wall, the hour finally came to an end. I looked at my watch and sighed with disappointment. My watch was the only thing my father left me besides memories and a brother on the Los Angeles Police Department. It ticked away happily, seldom coming within hours of the right time of day. Whenever I tried to reset it, it danced away energetically, like Luna.

"I'm afraid it's time," I said.

I held up my hand for Lou to stop playing. He capped the chorus with a flourish.

"So, I did?. . ."

". . . fine," I finished.

The moment had come for which I had been paid two hundred dollars up front by Fred Astaire. I followed as Luna's tap heels and toes clicked to the table, her towel, and her waiting water.

"You think Fred will . . . you know, like it?" she asked.

"He'll be knocked off his feet," I said.

"Do not overdo it, Peters," she said softly. "I am no dummy."

"Listen," I said, rubbing my hands together. "Mr. Astaire is working night and day on the defense-bond show for this

Saturday and then he won't be back from this war-bond tour for at least a month and . . ."

"You will work with me. Double the lessons. I will be dancing like Ginger when he gets back," she said.

"Right," I said.

"Wrong," she answered. "I want Fred Astaire. Period."

"Can I go?" Lou shouted across the room.

"Keep your skinny withered ass on that bench," Luna shouted.

"I'll give you a ride in a minute, Lou," I said.

"I can't hang around," he called.

"Are you deaf, you old fart?" Luna said.

"Give me five minutes, Lou," I called out. I took a breath and said to her, "Mr. Astaire won't be able to give you any more lessons. I'm sorry. He's sorry. After the tour, he starts rehearsing for another movie and then he . . ."

I didn't like the look on Luna's face.

"He teaches me to dance," she finished. It was not a request, or a question.

"'Fraid not," I said with a sigh. "Mr. Astaire gave you two lessons on Mr. Forbes's solicitation. During those lessons, you declared . . . let's say you indicated an attraction to Mr. Astaire."

"He is funny-looking," she said, her brown eyes unblinking. "But there is something sexy about him, you know?"

"Not really," I said. "No more lessons, Miss Martin. Mr. Astaire is happily married, has three children . . ."

"Two," she corrected, "one is adopted or something."

"Three," I insisted. "You need a teacher far more advanced than I am. I'm sure Mr. Astaire will be glad to find you a first-rate teacher who he will personally pay for, but . . ."

"No buts," she said, handing me the towel. "Here. You are sweating."

I was. I wiped my face. The towel smelled of Luna Martin. I felt just a little dizzy.

"I'm afraid I've been given the go-ahead by Mr. Astaire to tell Mr. Forbes about your attempted seduction of Mr. Astaire unless you agree to taking lessons from someone else."

She laughed. "Arthur will never believe you, or Astaire. I will call him a liar. Arthur will be very hurt. He will assume, with a little help from me, that Fred Astaire did not want to associate with me because of Arthur's reputation. Not only will Arthur be hurt, he will certainly be very angry."

She was almost in my face now.

"You want me to come back, you get a piano tuner in here," said Lou. "I can try to fix it myself, but . . ."

"Something wrong here?" a man's voice came from the general direction of the ballroom door.

"No, honey," Luna said, her face tauntingly close to mine, her lips within touching distance. "I was just considering giving Mr. Peters a thank-you kiss for a wonderful lesson."

"I don't think . . . "Arthur Forbes began.

Luna gave me a peck on the mouth, crinkled her nose fetchingly, and whispered, "Arthur gets very jealous."

She backed away and I faced the advancing Arthur. He was not big, about my height, five-ten or so and about twenty pounds heavier. Maybe two hundred or a little less. He was wearing a gray suit that looked new, and a shirt and tie that were definitely silk. His hair was brushed back, a little gray, a little long. I knew he was over sixty, but I wasn't sure how far over. There was nothing that hit you about his face except his eyes. They were big. They were blue. And they fixed on me with suspicion.

Behind him in the ballroom doorway stood a mass of a man, an Indian, in a perfectly pressed blue suit and tie. His thick hair was white, in contrast with his dark skin. He looked familiar, but I didn't have time to think about it.

"I'm gonna make this quick," Forbes said with a smile I didn't care for.

He held out his right hand. I shook it.

"My name is Forbes, Arthur. I'm a businessman."

Lou, ambling toward our happy trio and now within earshot, let out a laugh.

Forbes lost his smile and turned his eyes on the old man.

"Peters, Toby. I'm a dancer."

"You don't look like any dancer I've ever seen," said Forbes, turning his attention back to me.

"And you look like a businessman?" Lou said, joining our group.

"Go over in the corner for a few minutes, Grandpa," Forbes said, putting his right hand on Lou's shoulder. "The dancer here and me have something private to talk about."

"The old guy is senile or something," Luna said in what may have been real exasperation.

I looked at Luna. She had changed shoes and packed her things in a big red leather bag she had slung over her shoulder. She was resting her well-shaped behind against the table and clearly enjoying the scene.

"I've got a better idea, Mr. Fingers," said Lou. "Tell the human door over there to move out of the way so I can get to the bathroom."

"You should talk less, old man," Forbes said evenly.

"I should move my bowels more," said Lou. "I'm an old man, Mr. Fingers. I was married with two kids when Teddy Roosevelt got elected. I've played for and with the best for kings, movie stars, and, back in Detroit in '29 and '30, for gangsters . . ."

"I said you talk too much, piano man."

Lou shrugged and said, "You can't threaten me. I'm too old to care. But you're right. I talk too much. Someone fixing that piano and a few successful minutes in the bathroom can greatly improve my disposition."

Forbes was defeated. He snorted quietly and raised his left hand. The mountain in the doorway moved and Lou shuffled toward the john.

"What was just going on?" Forbes said.

"A dance lesson. Miss Martin is a very promising student."

Forbes looked at me with contempt.

"I've danced with her," he whispered. "Don't lie to me. I've got a built-in lie detector, a short attention span, and Kudlap over there, who has no sense of humor."

"Kudlap Singh?" I asked. "The Beast of Bombay?"

Forbes nodded and looked at his watch. I had seen Singh wrestle when I was a kid. My father took me and my brother, Phil, to boxing matches about three or four times a year. Once in a while, if Man Mountain Dean or the Beast of Bombay were on the card, we would go to the Garden for a night of choreographed groaning and blood.

"He must be sixty, maybe seventy," I said.

"You want to go shake hands with him?" Forbes said.

I looked at the Beast of Bombay and decided against trying to strike up a friendship.

"Arthur," Luna said impatiently. "Can we go?"

"You touch her again," he said, putting a finger very close to my left nostril, "and it's a toss-up whether you're playing piano with your knuckles or Kudlap rips your nose off."

"I don't play the piano," I said.

"Now's not a good time to take it up," Forbes said raising an eyebrow.

"Arthur," Luna said with the impatient sigh of someone trying to train a cat, "you have to touch if you are going to dance. Besides, I want Fred Astaire back. You promised, and where is he?"

"Practicing for a defense-bond show Saturday and getting ready for a war-bond drive," I repeated. "He'll be gone a long time, a month, maybe two. And when he comes back, he has a movie and . . ."

"We've got tickets for the show," Forbes said. "Wiltern Theater. When does he start giving Luna lessons again?"

It was my turn to sigh.

"Never," I said. "He asked me to tell you that he was considering opening a Fred Astaire Dance Studio, that Miss Martin would be given a full course at no charge." The dance studio idea had just come to me in a stroke of desperation.

"I want Fred Astaire," she said.

"She wants Astaire," Forbes said, closing the discussion.

"Right," I said. "She wants him in a bed."

Forbes's fists clenched and his face went red.

"He's lying, Arthur," Luna said calmly. "Astaire just doesn't want to teach me."

"You know who I am?" Forbes said.

"Arthur Forbes, businessman."

Forbes shook his head. This was going to be harder than he thought, and it might even ruin his morning.

"Dancer," he said, putting his hand on my right shoulder. "Do you know who I am?"

"Fingers Intaglia," I said.

"Do you know what I can do to Fred Astaire, and you?"

"I have an active imagination. And, by the way, I'm not a dancer. I'm a private investigator. My agency's been hired to see to it that Mr. Astaire doesn't have to give dance lessons to Miss Martin or anyone else."

"Private inv . . . you made all that up," screamed Luna. "You made me look like a . . . *Arthur!*"

"I've got to tell you, I don't like when Luna gets upset," Forbes said, squeezing my shoulder, his thumb expertly finding a nerve just below my collarbone. "When she is upset, she is not responsive. I want Luna happy. I want Luna responsive."

"Sounds good to me," I said, "but no more lessons with Fred Astaire. Let's make it easy, shake hands, walk away, and let Mr. Astaire find Miss Martin a terrific teacher. Look at it this way, she's had two lessons with Fred Astaire. Not many people can say that. It's a great start and . . ."

"I want Astaire," Luna said evenly.

"She wants Astaire," Forbes repeated.

"I'm sorry," I said. "Would you mind taking your hand off my shoulder?"

He squeezed a little harder.

"Right here, tomorrow, same time. Astaire is here. Show or no show. Bond drive. No bond drive."

"The hell with it," Lou said, inching past Kudlap in the doorway.

"Be quiet, old man," Forbes said without looking back at Lou.

"Be quiet?" said Lou, moving toward us. "My disposition has not been improved by my experience in the lavatory."

"Kudlap," Forbes called, and the Beast of Bombay, three hundred pounds, six-four or five and a stomach as flat as Death Valley, glided toward us like a cat.

"Old man," said Forbes as the Beast hovered over me. "I think you better leave or forget what you're gonna see next."

"My memory of yesterday is gone," Lou said with a sigh, "but ask me who played bass with King Oliver in '02 and I'll tell you his shoe size and how he liked his okra cooked for supper. I remember one night in Detroit when I was playing with Cookie Carmichael's band and someone who looked more than a little like you was having an argument with Kid Santini and . . ."

"Shut up, old man," Forbes said.

"Kid Santini turned up . . ." Lou tried, but Forbes said, "I said *shut up*."

Fingers Intaglia had a moment of doubt. He had come into the ballroom of his own hotel, expecting to pick up his girl. Instead he was facing a more than slightly wacky private detective and a what-the-hell-can-you-do-to-me old piano player. He took his hand from my shoulder. I wanted to rub where he had pressed, but I didn't.

"Tomorrow, right here. Astaire."

Forbes had taken a step back. He was bouncing slowly on his heels, considering his next move, when I said, "Mr. Astaire won't . . ."

"Don't say it again," Forbes cut in. "Something very bad will happen if you say it again. I strive for the patience of Thomas Jefferson, but I live with the temper of my sainted father, who ducked five manslaughter charges."

I shut up.

"Can we go now?" said Lou. "I'm working tonight at the Mozambique."

"Shut the old fool up, Arthur," Luna said, moving to Forbes's side and taking his arm.

"Give this message to Astaire," Forbes said, ignoring Lou and Luna both.

I looked at Luna. She was enjoying the moment. I almost missed Forbes's nod. I tightened up and started to turn. I was too late and the Beast of Bombay was too fast. I expected the blow to come to the kidney. Instead there was a zap, a feeling of being hit by a jolt of electricity and then pain that almost sent me to the floor.

Forbes was a professional. I had to give him that. The Beast had done something my old man had never even considered. He had spanked me. One whip of his giant hand. A second or two of humiliation followed by who knows how many hours or days of searing pain.

Luna tittered and I did my best not to fall. I started to go down anyway. Kudlap Singh held me up.

"I've seen this stuff before," Lou said with a bored voice of an ancient mariner who has seen and done everything.

"Got the message, Peters?" Forbes said.

I wasn't sure I could speak. I nodded.

"Good," he said. "You're gonna be sitting on pillows and taking warm baths for a while. Accidents like this happen. Astaire could be dancing in concrete shoes. Tomorrow, right here."

Forbes walked toward the door with the air of a man who had put things in order for everyone. The Beast of Bombay looked down at me and nodded before he followed his boss out of the ballroom. Luna, still holding Forbes's arm, smiled, patted her behind, puckered her lips, and made a kissing sound. She clicked toward the door with Forbes, swinging her red purse.

When the three of them were clearly and certainly out of the room, Lou came to me and said, "For twenty-five bucks, who needs this?"

I exhaled and decided to try talking. "I thought you weren't afraid," I said, trying to ignore the pain.

"I lied," Lou said. "Almost made in my pants. How are you doin'?"

"Could have been a lot worse if you weren't here. Thanks."

"A bonus is in order here," he said, helping me to the table Luna had abandoned.

I leaned against the table while Lou poured me an ice water. He filled the glass. I drank it all.

"Twenty-five bucks," I said.

"I'm satisfied," said Lou. "Now, how about a ride to Glendale?"

"I've got someone you should meet," I said, moving slowly toward the door. "I think you and my landlady might hit it off."

Lou shrugged. "I'm in the market," he said.

We made it out of the Monticello and to my khaki Crosley in the Monticello parking lot. When I had driven into the lot earlier, the attendant, a young guy about twenty-five with a decided limp, had looked at me as if my car was carrying a highly communicable automobile disease. Lou and I had watched him park it deep in the back of the lot, quarantined along with a slightly battered Hudson where the two cars were unlikely to infect the huddled Packards, Cadillacs, Lincolns, Chryslers, and a sleek black Graham parked up front where people would see them.

"How much?" I asked the kid. He was square-faced, in a clean blue uniform, and couldn't keep his hair out of his eyes.

"You a veteran?" he asked.

"No, but I feel like one. I've got a bad back, a sore ass, I'm pushing fifty, and I've got somewhere to go."

Lou ignored the two of us and headed for the car.

"He can't do that," the attendant said. "I get the cars."

"He's old and he's hard to stop."

"He a W-W-One veteran?"

"More likely the war with Spain," I said.

"All right, then," the attendant said. "Since he's a veteran, you get the discount."

"Thanks."

"Forty cents," he said, holding out his hand.

I fished out a buck, put it in his palm, and said, "Keep the change. You a veteran?"

"I was on the *Yorktown* when it got hit by the Japs. Never forget the day. Two in the afternoon. I was on deck. Fires all over the place from the thirty, maybe forty Jap dive bombers, torpedo planes from the *Hiryu*."

The kid's eyes were glazed and far away, off the coast of Midway on a June afternoon a little less than a year ago.

"Caught flying metal in the leg," the attendant said, touching his right leg. "And my head. Mom's got the shrapnel from my leg and my medal on the fireplace right under Jesus. I'm still lugging iron up here."

He tapped on his head.

"Glad you're okay now—?"

"Cotton," he said, holding out his hand. "Cotton Wright."

"Toby Peters."

He nodded as if he expected me to be named Toby Peters and then he limped off to get my Crosley.

It was Thursday, March 11, 1943. The Japanese were bombing Guadalcanal. Our planes had hit the Japs at Balle in the Shortland Islands. General Sir Bernard L. Montgomery said Rommel was desperate in Tunisia, and the Royal Air Force had hit Munich hard with five-hundred-ton blockbuster bombs. Roosevelt had just proposed a birth-to-grave Social Security that included medical care and payments for college education.

The war was getting long and I was getting twenty-five dollars a day plus expenses to convince a daffy woman and a semiretired gangster to leave Fred Astaire alone.

Cotton Wright pulled the Crosley next to me and crawled out of the door, which wasn't easy. The Crosley could hold a driver and a passenger if they didn't mind bending over like clowns packing into one of those circus cars.

"Thanks, Cotton," I said, trying to ease into the driver's seat.

The burning from Kudlap Singh's whack grew close to unbearable as my rear end hit the seat. I eased down, gritting my teeth, and closed the door. I was sweating and starting to imagine the rare and exotic pain that I could bring to Fingers Intaglia.

I waved to Cotton as we pulled into the traffic on Sunset.

"Glendale," Lou said.

"Glendale," I agreed.

Chapter Two

I Wanna Be a Dancing Man

The whole thing had started two days earlier, a little before eleven in the morning, when I went to my office. The Farraday is downtown on Hoover, just off Ninth. I was in a good mood. I'd just finished two tacos, a couple of cups of coffee, and a sinker at Manny's on the corner. That was my early lunch. I could afford it. I had a little over two hundred dollars left of a fee from Clark Gable.

I had paid off my fifteen-dollar rent for March and the advance on April to my landlady. Mrs. Plaut had tucked it into her dress next to her unample bosom. I had also paid two months' advance rent on the closet I used for an office and sublet from Sheldon Minck, D.D.S. I had a cupboard full of Wheaties and no overly demanding aches or pains.

Life was good. I entered the Lysol-smelling outer lobby of the Farraday and checked the board to be sure I was still listed. There I was, in neatly typed letters, Toby Peters, Private Investigator, Room 602. Above me on the board was Anthony Pelligrino, Matters of the Heart and Certified Public Accountant. I had never met Anthony. Below me on the board was Quick Work Loans, whose motto, I had discovered from a one-sheet flyer shoved under our office door, was, "You Need It, We Give It, You Pay Back in Small Installments." The flyer had also assured me that Barbara and Daniel Sullivan would give me "sympathy and fast results." The rest of the board was a full spectrum of the down-and-out and vaguely sinister. One-room talent agencies, fortune-tellers, baby photographers, publishers of questionable literature, a vocal teacher, a music teacher (Professor Aumont of the Paris International Academy of Music), who guaranteed to teach you any instrument in one month, and Good Jewelry, so named not because of the quality of the merchandise but the name of the seldom-seen proprietor, Herschel Good. This was not Sunset Boulevard. I went through the door leading to the semidarkness of the inner lobby. The inner chamber of the building was vast, the offices on each floor opening out onto a landing. A few steps out your door and you were at the iron railing from which you could look up or down into the echoing and sometimes noisy heart of the Farraday.

I looked up as I headed for the staircase. If my back wasn't bothering me I avoided the ancient, groaning elevator in the darkest corner next to the stairs. Through its prisonlike bars, the elevator provided a good view of each floor as it slowly rose. The key word here is *slowly*.

Somewhere on two a woman was either being murdered or trying to sing. On three there was laughter, very insincere male laughter, lots of it. But mostly there was the wall-dulled sound of people's voices. You couldn't hear the words, but you could hear begging, pleading, lying, hope, and sometimes pain. The sound of pain grew louder as I got to the sixth floor and headed for my office. On the pebbled glass was:

Sheldon Minck, D.D.S., S.D.
Dentist
Toby Peters
Private Investigator

Behind the door someone was moaning, the gender of the source unclear. I stepped in. The little waiting room—and calling it *little* is giving it the benefit of the doubt—had been converted into a reception area with two small chairs and a desk that barely deserved the name. On the desk was a telephone and a pad of paper. Behind the desk was Violet Gonsenelli, the receptionist Shelly had hired in spite of my warnings. The problem wasn't Violet. Violet was fun to look at, about twenty-five, pretty, with a pale face and dark hair piled perfect and high on her head. She wore a white nursing uniform and an instant smile when the door was opened. Violet's husband was a rising middleweight. He had moved as high as number six in the *Ring Magazine* ratings before he got drafted. Both Violet and a shot at the title would have to wait till the war was over. The other problem was Mildred Minck, wife of Sheldon Minck, a woman of little tolerance and even less charm. Mildred rarely came to the office. She didn't like the smell of alcohol and wintergreen and she didn't like me. And she didn't think all that much of Sheldon.

Somehow Shelly had convinced Mildred that he needed a receptionist/assistant, and Mildred had agreed. That should have made Shelly Minck suspicious. It made me suspicious, but that, when I am working, is part of my job.

"Mr. Peters," Violet said, all business, picking up her pad. "You have calls. A Mrs. Eastwood . . ."

"Former landlady, claims I owe her for damage to the room I rented," I explained. "That was four, five years ago. Bad news."

"Anne," she went on. "She said you'd know who she was."

"Good news, maybe. Former wife. That was more than four or five years ago. You remind me a little of Anne when she was your age. But Anne had a lot more . . ."

Violet tore off the top sheet of her pad and handed it to me. I folded it once neatly.

The groan from beyond the inner door tore through me.

"Dr. Minck has a patient," Violet whispered as if we were in a sick room or the Burbank Library. "Very sensitive."

"Sounds it," I said. "I have two questions, Violet."

She folded her hands in front of her, and her red lips pouted seriously.

"First, how do you get through that narrow space to your desk, and second, what happened to the two chairs that Shelly moved into the hall for waiting patients to sit on?"

The idea was that Violet would have enough room to move her arms and other parts of her anatomy if patients waited outside.

"Chairs were stolen," she said sadly. "And I can scrunch myself all together and just make it, but I can't wear stockings. They'd snag. Not that I have the nylons to spare. But Doctor Minck says he knows where to get real silk stockings. He said he'd like to see me wearing silk stockings to work. It relaxes the patients."

"I doubt it," I said as a shriek of agony froze my spine. "Doesn't that bother you, Violet?"

"No," she said pertly. "My father was a light heavyweight. I love the fights. That's how I met my husband. I'm used to pain and brutality."

"I'm a fight fan too," I said.

"Maybe we could go together sometime," she said brightly.

"I don't think that would be a good idea."

She shrugged.

"Who do you figure in the Ortiz-Salica fight tomorrow?" I asked. Mexican Manuel Ortiz and Lou Salica of Brooklyn were battling for the bantamweight championship in Oakland.

"Ortiz," Violet said. "It won't go the distance."

"Salica's got heart," I said.

"Ortiz has a right hand and fast feet," she said, searching her desk drawer for something.

"Bet you lunch at Manny's," I said.

She found the pencil she was looking for, shrugged, and said, "Okay."

"You like the job so far?" I said, reluctant to open the inner door and face whatever mayhem Sheldon was doling out to what may or may not have been an innocent patient.

"Not too many patients, not too many calls. Plenty of time to read and learn." She opened a drawer in the little desk and in the small space behind the drawer wiggled out two books. "Dental hygiene and Spanish. Dr. Minck thinks there's a whole new market of Mexicans out there," she said with a wave of her hand. "Somewhere. Oh, God. I almost forgot. You've got someone in your office waiting for you. It couldn't be, but I think it's a movie star. You know the goofy one with the fat partner?"

It sounded like a description of me and Shelly.

"Laurel. Stan Laurel," she said.

"Waiting in my office?"

"He didn't give his name."

I went through the inner door, closed it behind me, and found myself face to face with the rotund rear of Sheldon Minck draped in soiled white dental smock, as he huddled over someone.

"Almost. Almost. Almost," Shelly chanted.

A pair of legs, female, squirmed, and their possessor whimpered in defeat.

"There. Hah. There," Shelly said with a deep sigh, turning to look in my direction. In his right hand was a narrow pliers. Clutched in the mouth of the pliers was a bloody tooth. There were spatters of red on the front of Shelly's smock and a look of triumph on his round, perspiring face. His thick glasses had slipped to the end of his nose and the few wisps of hair that still clung to the top of his head danced crazily.

He displayed the bloody tooth to the woman in the chair, who seemed to have passed out.

Shelly didn't appear to notice. He dropped pliers and tooth on the little porcelain-top table next to the dental chair. He picked up the stump of a cigar from the table and placed it triumphantly and as yet unlit in the corner of his mouth.

"You should have seen it, Toby," he said, fishing under his smock for matches. "Molar, almost impacted. Bad shape. Could have crumbled. And you know what that means?"

He found a match and lit the cigar.

"She fainted, Shel," I said.

Shelly turned to the patient, squinted through his thick glasses.

"She's breathing fine," he said, turning back to me. "How do you like the office?"

I looked around. Violet had begun a major campaign against a decade's worth of filth. There were no coffee mugs or dishes piled in the sink. There was nothing at all in the sink, in fact, it was clean. The trash can was not overflowing and had a cover on it. Magazines were no longer strewn over cabinets and counters. The yellow linoleum floor was spotless, except for the few splotches of blood from Shelly's very recent triumph.

Violet had also put a painting on the wall to cover a bulging crack. The painting showed Napoleon, a sword in his right hand, on top of a white horse that was rearing back with his two front legs high in the air. Behind Napoleon were a bunch of soldiers in uncomfortable-looking uniforms, following him into battle.

"You've got a visitor," Shelly whispered slyly.

"Stan Laurel," I said.

"Violet told you," he said. "Tell him I give a major discount to your clients."

"No," I said. "I don't want you to talk to my clients, let alone work on their teeth."

"I'm good, Toby. You know I'm good."

"You're fine, Shelly. I just don't think it's right to mix business with torture. I think you should do something about your patient. She's a funny shade of orange."

With that I turned to my office, a space just a little bit larger than Violet's reception room. I tried not to see clients in the office. Most of my jobs were set up by phone calls. Not too many people stumbled on my office in the dark halls of the sixth floor of the Farraday while they were on the way to a music lesson and said to themselves, "Hey, a private detective. Wife's been gone for a month. That is just what I need."

Even if such an event did take place, few people would be filled with confidence by a private investigator who could only be reached by going through a dental office.

I opened my office door, and Fred Astaire turned in his chair. I closed the door behind me.

"They said . . ." I began, shaking his hand as he stood.

"That I was Stan Laurel. I heard. Not all that unusual a mistake. I've got to confess that sometimes when I look in the mirror I could swear Laurel was on the other side."

"Cup of coffee?" I asked, moving behind my desk and clearing away three days of mail to make room for the sheet from Violet's pad with Anne's number on it.

"No, thanks," said Astaire.

There was one window in the room. Right behind the desk. Perfect view of the alley six flights below. If I leaned out, I could see my Crosley parked between the garbage cans. I opened the window, sat, and faced Astaire, who was wearing a perfectly tailored blue suit, an off-blue shirt, and a tie the color of the suit. He looked a little skinnier than he did in the movies, no more than one-forty, and he was about my height, maybe five-nine. I figured him for about forty, maybe a little older. He had less hair than I remembered, and the memory wasn't that old. I'd taken Carmen, the cashier at Levy's on Spring, to see *You Were Never Lovelier* about a month ago.

"Yes," he said.

"Yes?" I repeated.

"The hair, or lack of it," Astaire said. "You were looking at my head. In the movies, I wear a wig. I hate the damn thing. In public, I wear a hat."

He held up a hat he had apparently placed on the floor.

"While I'd say I'm a reasonably presentable example of the human male," he went on, "were I not a movie actor, I doubt if women would notice me on the street."

I assumed we were getting somewhere, so I shut up. He continued: "You were recommended to me as someone who could be . . . discreet."

"I can be discreet," I assured him.

He nodded and looked around the room.

"I know the style's not right," he said, looking at the painting on the wall to his right. "Too naturalistic. But I'd almost swear it was a Dali."

"It is," I said. "Payment for a job I did for him."

The painting showed a woman with a warm, loving face holding two little naked boy babies, one in each arm.

"Amazing," said Astaire. "Aren't you afraid . . . I mean, someone could . . ."

"Mr. Astaire . . ."

"Fred."

"Fred, if you were a robber and you made your way through Dr. Minck's office back here with a flashlight in your hand, do you think you'd recognize the painting as anything worth stealing?"

"Probably not," he said.

"Besides, it's too big to sneak out."

"They could wrap it up, throw it out the window, and then go down the stairs and pick it up."

"You spend a lot of time hanging around criminals?" I said.

"Well, as a matter of fact, I do, which is part of the reason I'm here," he said softly. "I'm a bit of a police buff. No, I'm more than a bit. I'm fascinated by the police and the criminal world. I've gone out on patrols in almost every major city in the United States, and I go rather frequently out in police cars and to lineups. Phyllis sometimes joins me."

"Phyllis?"

"My wife. The people in the photograph . . ." he said, turning to look up past my investigator's license at the fading photo of a weathered man with two young boys at his side and a German shepherd at his feet.

"My father," I said. "Younger kid is me. Older one is my brother, Phil. The dog is Kaiser Wilhelm. My father and the dog are dead."

"The photograph rather echoes the Dali painting," he said. "A parent, two boys."

"Never thought of it," I said.

"I never had much to do with my father," Astaire said. "My sister and my mother and I were out on the road by the time I was five. My father stayed in Omaha. Saw him once in a while but . . ."

The pause was long and he sighed.

"I'm stalling."

"I noticed," I said. "I'm in no hurry."

"There is a woman," he said, looking at the Dali painting. "She wanted dancing lessons from me. She approached me through a phone call from her 'friend,' an Arthur Forbes. You may know the name."

"I know the name," I said. "Also known as Fingers Intaglia, from Detroit. Son-in-law of Guiseppi Cortona, who runs mob business in Minneapolis."

"Mr. Forbes was rather insistent that I teach his friend," Astaire went on. "Indicated that she wanted no other teacher, would accept no other teacher. He also said that his friend had, until recently, been a ballroom dance teacher, but she needed to move on to the heights of professionalism. I could name my own price but, as he put it, he would be 'very disappointed' if I refused. Mr. Peters . . . Toby, I have a wife and three children—the youngest, Ava, just had her first birthday. A father's nightmare is that something might happen to his family. A dancer's nightmare is that something might happen to his body. My knowledge of Mr. Forbes's history suggests that both nightmares might come true. I agreed to a limited number of lessons. Forbes set up a schedule with me at the Monticello Hotel."

"On Sunset."

"On Sunset," he confirmed. "I picked the times and brought my own accompanist. This is difficult. The young woman's name is Luna Martin. She is pretty. She is smart. She is not graceful, but she is determined. As I said, she also claims to have been a dance instructor. One can only guess at the number of lead-footed zombies she unleashed on the dance floors of America. At the end of the second lesson last Thursday, when the piano player was taking a break, Miss Martin unbuttoned her silk blouse, displayed her considerable breasts, and declared that she wanted me and was determined to have me."

I nodded.

Music was now coming from Shelly's office. It sounded like the Modernaires.

"I've been in vaudeville, musical comedy, and movies all my life," said Astaire. "I've seen bare-breasted women and have been approached by a variety of females who have made it clear that they were available. I am quite happily married and inclined neither to couple with Luna Martin nor be deformed by her boyfriend. In short . . ."

"You want me to find a way to get her off your back."

"And every other part of my anatomy," he amended. "Miss Martin expects her next lesson Thursday morning at ten. I can make an excuse and skip this one. Maybe I can even make a reasonable excuse and miss two sessions. Three would sorely challenge my limited verbal skill, and four would be impossible."

"I get rid of Luna Martin and Forbes, and I provide you with protection. That it?" I said, taking notes on the back of one of the many envelopes on my desk.

"At least till the situation is reasonably safe," he said. "Is this a reasonable request?"

"Twenty-five a day for me, plus expenses. Twenty per man for protection. I think we're talking about two or three men for a few weeks at least. Or you can go one hundred a day and I cover the cost of additional help. Of course, you get a detailed accounting."

"It could run into money," Astaire said, rubbing his chin thoughtfully.

"It could," I agreed.

"Considering the amount I've lost on the horses," he said, standing, "I think it's a wise investment. One condition. No police. No publicity."

"No police. No publicity. No guarantee, but I'll do my best."

I held out my hand and he took it.

"I need one more thing from you," I said.

"An advance," he said, reaching for his wallet.

"That would be nice," I said. "But what I really need is one quick dance lesson so I can take your place at the Monticello Thursday."

"Can you dance at all?"

"Not a step," I said.

He sighed deeply, took out his wallet, and gave me two hundred dollars in cash, saying he didn't want to use checks for this. He also gave me a private phone number where I could reach him and told me to meet him at R.K.O. the next morning, Wednesday, for an emergency dance lesson.

"I've heard I can rely on you," Astaire said, taking the doorknob in hand.

I nodded with a knowing smile and more confidence than I felt, and Fred Astaire opened the door, letting in the voices of the Modernaires before he left.

In the dental office, I could hear Shelly speaking quickly to Astaire. I couldn't make out the words. The door to the reception room opened and closed and I knew that Astaire had made his escape.

As soon as I knew he was safe, I flattened out the sheet of paper Violet had given me and put in a call to Anne.

Anne and I had been divorced for more than six years. She had stayed with me when I was a cop in Glendale and a security guard at Warner Brothers. When I got fired from Warners by Jack Warner himself, for breaking the nose of a cowboy star who wouldn't keep his hands off a girl in the accounting office, Anne had said I would never grow up. She was right, I guess. I loved her. She left me. From time to time, when my hard head could help her out of a tight spot, she gave me a call.

I didn't recognize the number. I reached for the phone, gave the operator the number. A woman, not Anne, answered after the first ring.

"Rappeneau and Darin," she said.

"Anne Mitzenmacher," I said.

"I'm sorry, sir, but we have no Anne Mitzenmaker."

"Mitzen*mach*er," I corrected.

"No one with a name anything like that," she said.

"Do you have an Anne anything?"

"Anne Peters," she said.

"That's the one," I said.

She couldn't help saying, "Peters doesn't sound anything like . . . I'll connect you."

Another ring and Anne picked up the phone, saying, "Anne Peters, can I help you?"

Anne had a deep, lush voice that brought memories of her soft, dark hair, her large lips, her large everything.

"You're using my name," I said lightly.

"My options are limited," she said. "It's easier for the clients to remember, and I doubt if the receptionist could even say Mitzenmacher."

"She can't. I tried her. What are you selling, Anne?"

"Houses," she said. "This is a real-estate company. We're on Washington, just off Highland."

After Anne divorced me she had married Ralph, an airline executive. Life was good. Home on Malibu Beach. Then Ralph made some mistakes with the wrong people and wound up dead and broke.

"You called to beg my forgiveness and tell me you can't live without me," I said.

"No jokes, Toby, please."

"I was hoping, Anne."

"You never remember the bad times."

"That's one of my strengths," I said.

"And I'm doomed to remember them all," she said. "One of my weaknesses. I'd like your help."

"You've got it."

"Don't you want to hear what it is first?"

"No," I said.

"Can you meet me for lunch? Noon, there's a restaurant called Roth's on Fifth near Olive . . ."

"By the Biltmore Hotel. I know it. I'll be there."

"You're not working, or? . . ."

"As a matter of fact, I'm working for Fred Astaire. He's giving me a dance lesson tomorrow."

"You don't change, Toby," Anne said with a sigh. "I've got to go. There's another call. Noon at Roth's."

I tucked the two fifties and five twenties into my wallet. With the two hundred I had hidden in an envelope behind the Beech-Nut Gum clock on the wall of my room at Mrs. Plaut's boardinghouse, I now had a little over four hundred dollars and all my bills paid.

It was Tuesday morning. Life was still just fine.

If I hurried I could just make it to Roth's by noon with a few minutes to spare. I left my office and attempted a quick retreat across the no-man's-land of Sheldon Minck's office.

"Did you talk to him?" Shelly said, stopping me just short of the door. "About my working on his teeth?"

"I told you I wouldn't, Shel," I said, turning to face him and the woman in the chair, who appeared to be just coming out of shock. Her eyes were blinking and she was looking around, trying to remember where she was.

"Not fair, Toby. I tell all my patients who need a private detective that help is right across the office."

"You've never sent me a client, Shel."

"I've had very few patients who needed a detective," he said, removing his cigar so he could examine it for signs of possible betrayal before he lit it. "Mr. Laurel needs dental work."

"That wasn't Stan Laurel," I said. "It was Fred Astaire."

Shelly returned the cigar to his mouth, wiped his hands on

his smock, and blew smoke in the direction of his bewildered patient.

"Vera, Mrs. Davis, was the man who just walked through here Fred Astaire?"

Mrs. Davis looked around for someone who might resemble Fred Astaire. All she could see were me and Shelly. She tried to sit up, a look of pain double-crossed her face, and she let out a fresh groan.

"See," said Shelly triumphantly. "She's fine."

"I've got to go, Shel," I said.

"Tell Violet I need her in here."

In the reception room of Minck and Peters, I told Violet that the good dentist needed her in surgery. Violet inched her way from behind her desk and through the narrow space between it and the wall.

"I'll call later," I said.

She popped out from the side of the desk and said, "Ortiz, and it won't go the distance."

I was out the door and into the hallway outside our office. Still plenty of time, though I couldn't check it on a reliable watch. Six floors below, the voices of two men were echoing loud and dirty. I moved along the railing toward the stairs and looked down. The bald head and the burly body told me that one of the three men below was the Farraday's owner, Jeremy Butler. I didn't recognize the two men with him, at least not from this angle, but they were big and standing close to Jeremy.

I started down the stairs, unable to sort the words of anger from their echo.

Jeremy is pushing sixty-five, or maybe pulling it. He's an ex-wrestler who saved his money and wound up with a second-rate office building and some scattered third-rate apartment buildings. He was now a landlord with time to devote to his passion—poetry—and to his family, which included his wife, the former Alice Pallis, who nearly matched Jeremy in size and strength, and their one-year-old daughter, Natasha, a curly-haired beauty who bore no resemblance to either of her parents.

By the time I made it down to the lobby, I could see the two men shouting in Jeremy's face. One was young, no more than thirty. Giving him the benefit of the doubt he looked a little like a crazed John Garfield. The other was in his forties and looked a little like a pig. The pig held something in his right hand, something metal.

"You'll pay," the older one was saying. "You hear me?"

Jeremy didn't answer. He looked from one to the other with his hands at his sides.

"Everybody's paying, up and down the street," the younger one shouted.

"I will advise them not to do so," Jeremy said softly.

"There are bad people around the city," the older one said. "Vandals. People who destroy other people's property for no reason. They break windows and . . . I've told you this already. You're not listening."

I paused at the bottom step, fairly sure they couldn't see me. Then I saw that the object in the older guy's hand was a small crowbar. I took a step out of the shadows. The younger one spotted me and nudged his partner, who looked toward me.

"You a cop?" he asked cautiously.

"No," I said.

"Then stay out of this," he warned, holding up the crowbar. "This is a business discussion with the old man."

"I was just going to ask for the time," I said.

"It's eleven-twenty, Toby," Jeremy said.

The crowbar came up in a streak. So did Jeremy's left hand. He grabbed the older guy's wrist and twisted. The one who looked like John Garfield started to throw a punch. Jeremy swooped the arm he was holding right at the younger guy, and the crowbar, still in the hand of the pig, hit John Garfield in the face. The younger guy staggered back with a yell, his hands covering his eyes. Jeremy let go of the wrist of the other man, who went down on his knees in agony. The crowbar clattered to the floor and the man's wrist hung limp and possibly broken.

I watched while Jeremy advanced on the man who had taken the crowbar across his face, now backed up against the wall. He took his hands down, blood streaming from his nose, a look of panic in his eyes.

"Don't touch your nose," Jeremy said, reaching up for the man's face. "This will hurt but the bone will be back in place, and if you don't touch it, it will heal and look quite natural."

Before the man could mount a protest, Jeremy put his left hand behind the man's head and pinched his nose between the thumb and fingers of his right hand. The man squirmed, let out an anguished "Ahhhhhh," and sank to the floor.

Jeremy turned to the man with the injured wrist, who was trying to stand.

"Hey, enough," the man said. "Me and Twines are just trying to make a living here."

Jeremy moved toward him.

"The truth is nobody on the block gave us money," the man said. "The truth is we're no damn good at this and getting pretty goddamn frustrated. Twines is my sister's kid. How am I gonna explain his broken nose?"

Jeremy didn't answer. He grabbed the man's shoulder and held up the damaged arm. The man tried to pull away.

"It's not broken," Jeremy said. "Sprained wrist. Go."

"I want my crowbar."

"I suggest you listen to the man," I said.

The man with the sprained wrist winced his way to his

nephew, who was trying to get up from his knees. He put his good arm around Twines and said, "This is a goddamn hard life, let me tell you."

"Go, now," Jeremy said gently.

The two men slouched to the door, went into the outer lobby, and out onto Hoover in search of a new line of work.

"This is no longer a safe neighborhood," Jeremy said as he bent to pick up the crowbar.

"It's not a safe world," I added.

"I have a wife and child," he said, looking around the vast lobby of his office building and up toward the offices on the eighth floor he had converted to a rambling apartment for his family.

"Might be a good idea to . . . I'm on my way to a real-estate dealer I know. You want me to? . . ."

"No, thank you, Toby," he said, surveying the trail of blood from Twines's nose. "I have other property."

"I'm late, Jeremy," I said.

"If you have some time later, I have a new poem."

"Later, promise," I said, en route to the door.

It was still a good day.

I went out the rear exit of the Farraday and headed for my car. The open lot was covered with gravel; trash, which Jeremy cleaned up once a week, thrown from the windows of the Farraday; and the wreckage of two abandoned cars in which, depending on the season, a homeless alcoholic or two resided. This season's resident of the alley was Vince. Vince was standing in front of my Crosley. I had paid Vince a quarter, the going rate, for watching my car. The possible dangers to my car were theft, stolen tires or hubcaps, broken windows, and Vince.

Vince looked somewhere near sixty but was probably closer to forty-five. He had a reasonably clean-shaven face with a few nicks and healing cuts. I had given him a Gillette razor, a pack of Blue blades, two of my old shirts, an antique pair of pants I found in the back of my closet, and a pair of university oxfords that had always pinched my toes. I had also suggested to him that he put on the clothes, shave, and make the rounds of the local restaurants in search of a pearl-diving job.

It had worked for the last keeper of the alley.

Vince had solemnly promised he would make the rounds, but when it came to actually going into a diner and asking to see the boss, it was too much for him, or so he had told me with a shrug.

"A man's nature is a man's nature," Vince had said with a sigh.

Vince said he had been a history teacher in a high school in Chicago until he fell or was pushed down a school stairway between classes. The world had gone blurry, and only a drink or twenty could make it seem clear again. He had been fired in the middle of a semester and, since he had no family, Vince had packed his bag, got into his car, and driven out in search of a cave or hole to hide in. That, Vince said, was "five or six or eight years ago, certainly long before this war and long after the last one."

I handed Vince two quarters and said thanks.

He looked at the two quarters and handed one back to me.

"My fee was a quarter," he said. "This is business, not charity."

"You might want to raise your rates a little," I suggested, opening the Crosley's door. "Prices are going up everywhere. I think your customers would understand."

"You are my only customer," Vince said, pocketing the quarter in what used to be my pants. "Now, if you want to put me on an exclusive retainer and continue to pay at the current rate . . ."

I turned awkwardly in my seat, fished a dollar bill from

my wallet, and handed it to him. It followed the quarter into his pocket.

"We should have a written contract," Vince said.

"Write it up. I'll sign it."

I closed the door, waved good-bye, turned on the radio, and drove out of the alley. I took Main the few blocks to Washington, where I made a right turn and went straight to Highland.

Morton Downey sang me down the street with Raymond Paige's Orchestra backing him up. Downey finished a tearful chorus of "Danny Boy" and then tried to sell me some Coca-Cola. Pepsi's my drink and, once in a while, a beer or two or three, but I'd almost cried at the end of "Danny Boy," so I promised Morton I'd have a Coke with lunch.

I had no trouble finding a parking space on Fifth and I walked into Roth's with about two minutes to spare, according to the clock on the wall. It was lunchtime for the insurance companies, lawyers' firms, shopkeepers, and clerks in the neighborhood. The place was noisy, crowded, and smelled of hot pastrami.

Anne sat at a small table near the kitchen door. Her hands were folded in front of her. Her eyes met mine. No smile. All business. Not what I wanted to see. I weaved my way through the tables, pulled out a chair across from Anne, and sat. She was wearing a brown twill suit, and she had lost some weight. She was dark and more beautiful and serious than I had remembered.

"Thanks for coming, Toby," she said.

A fizzing glass of dark liquid sat in front of me, a cup of coffee in front of Anne.

"My pleasure," I said, meaning it.

"I ordered you a Pepsi," she said, gesturing at the drink before me.

"Thanks," I said, making a note to keep my Coke pledge to Morton Downey in the very near future.

"I ordered you a pastrami on rye with ketchup," she said. "If you . . ."

"Sounds perfect," I said over the clatter of trays and dishes and the ramble of voices around us.

"First," Anne said, looking at me with her warm brown eyes, "I want to thank you for keeping your promise."

I shrugged and drank my Pepsi.

About six months ago, give or take an hour, I had promised Anne I would stop dropping in at her apartment at all hours of the day or night, would not call her unless I had a real emergency, and would stop sending her poetry which, she said, was "obviously not written by you." I had, with the agony of a four-year-old who can't sit still for dinner, stayed away.

"You're looking good, Toby."

"You're looking beautiful, Anne."

"Thank you."

A skinny waitress in a wilting Betty Crocker of a uniform plunked our lunches in front of us and hurried away. Anne had vegetable soup and a salad. My hot pastrami came with a stack of fries. I should have been happy, but I knew something was about to be served that I wouldn't like. I took a bite of the sandwich. It was hot and piled high with thin slices of spiced meat. It didn't taste half bad for Los Angeles pastrami.

"How are Phil and . . ." Anne said after a nibble of lettuce.

"My brother is fine," I interrupted. "His wife and kids are fine. Sheldon Minck is fine. I've got about four hundred dollars. My back is holding up well. I'm seeing the cashier at Levy's. Her name is Carmen. She reminds me of you, without the smarts. I'm still in the boardinghouse. I still go to the fights when I can and . . ."

It was her turn to interrupt.

"Enough," Anne said, putting down her fork and meeting my eyes.

I took a determined third bite of my sandwich and washed it down with Pepsi.

"I'm going to get married," she said.

"Congratulations," I said. "Anyone I know?"

"You've seen him," she said, watching me eat. "I sold him a house. He made me laugh."

That hurt more than the news that Anne was getting married. I had made her smile a few dozen times when we were married, but no laughs. And I was sure there had been no laughs with her second husband, Ralph.

"Open the envelope and read the winner's name," I said between furious attacks on phase two of the sandwich.

"Preston Stewart," she said.

I didn't feel like eating any more. Preston Stewart was a contract player at M-G-M. Preston Stewart had been in about two-dozen movies and had starred in two low-budget ones, one a Western, the other a melodrama. He was blond, good-looking with lots of teeth, and, worst of all, he had to be a good ten years younger than Anne.

"Toby? Say something."

"I heard on the radio that the Chinese have begun translating the *Encyclopedia Britannica*. News came straight from Chungking. Middle of a war with Japs running all over their country and they're translating an encyclopedia. You can't beat people like that. You can only kill them."

"Toby, please," she said, gently but firmly.

"What am I supposed to say? I said congratulations. I love you. I want you back. I'm never going to get you. You're marrying a kid movie actor with . . . with teeth, lots of teeth, big white ones. And he can make you laugh."

"I'm sorry," she said, pushing her salad around with her fork, not eating.

"And that's why you called me?"

"I thought I should tell you face to face," she said.

The skinny waitress was back.

"Everything okay?" she asked, not much caring and reaching for my empty plate. The fries were gone. I had eaten them without knowing it.

"Fine," I said.

"Coffee?"

"Another Pepsi," I said.

"Just ran out of Pepsi. Coke or Royal Crown."

"Coke," I said.

"Coffee," Anne said, looking at her watch. "Black."

The waitress nodded and headed through the door to the kitchen.

"Would you like to know about Preston? It might make it easier if you knew what a . . ."

"No," I said, holding up a hand. "I don't want to know how kind, loving, rich, and funny he is. Call me a sore loser. Call me childish, which you've been known to do. My guess is I'll avoid Preston Stewart movies for a year and then I'll start going to all of them, looking for signs of decay or melting, wondering how you two hit it off in bed and if he's still keeping you laughing down on the beach in your tans."

"I didn't think you'd be this bitter," Anne said.

"You caught me by surprise. I didn't have time to fake it or tell a bad joke or two. The truth just came out."

The waitress was back with my Coke and Anne's coffee. She put the check in front of me. Anne reached over the table for it.

"I invited you to lunch," she said.

"Do me a favor," I said. "Let me come out of this with a little dignity. The bill's only two bucks and change."

Anne sat back, looked at her coffee, tucked away a wisp of hair behind her left ear, and looked back at me.

"I'm sorry," I said. "You deserve a break. I hope Preston Stewart is it."

"Thanks, Toby," she said.

"When's the wedding?"

"Soon. When . . . if you ever feel better about this, I'd like you to meet Press."

"One condition," I said. "I don't have to call him Press."

Anne almost smiled.

"His real name is Asher Cahn."

I nodded and finished my Coke. Anne hadn't touched her coffee.

"Thanks for caring enough to tell me face to face," I said, picking up the check.

"I don't think it would be a good idea to invite you to the wedding, Toby."

"It would be a very bad idea."

Anne dabbed at the corners of her mouth with her napkin and rose. So did I.

"I'm a little late," she said. "I've got to hurry."

I nodded and got up.

Anne came around the table, touched my hand, and kissed my cheek. I think she was crying. At least I like to think there was a tear or two. Then she was gone.

I left a big tip and was turning toward the cash register when the skinny waitress appeared, picked up the tip, and said, "She dump ya?"

"Yeah."

"Figures. She didn't eat and you leave a big tip."

"You should be a detective," I said.

"Helps to have a little knowledge of human nature in this job," she said. "Go get a little drunk. I do when I get dumped."

"I don't drink," I said.

She shrugged and answered the upheld hand of a distant customer.

Less than twenty minutes later I was at the Y.M.C.A. downtown on Hope Street. I looked for Doc Hodgdon or someone else for a handball game. No luck. So I got my stiff light gloves from my locker, loosened them up, and attacked the heavy punching bag in the corner of the gym, near an old guy with dyed red hair who was steadily shooting free throws.

After twenty minutes of punching and a shower, I felt tired and a little better. There was a Loew's theater a few blocks from the Y. I walked over and saw a March of Time about the New Canada and *They Got Me Covered* with Bob Hope. It was only a little after four when I got out and closed my eyes against the afternoon sun.

I got in my car and drove to the Roxy, where I saw *He's My Guy* with Joan Davis, Dick Foran, and the Mills Brothers. There was also a musical short with Borrah Minevitch's Original Harmonica Rascals. I remember the little guy, Johnny Puleo, wearing cowboy chaps and trying to muscle his way into the act. That's all I remember of what I had seen in the dark that day. Joan Davis and Bob Hope had gotten a few smiles out of me but that was it.

The sun was still up but not as bright and there was a chill in the air. I headed home. It was about dinnertime, but I wasn't hungry.

I found a space on Heliotrope about half a block down from Mrs. Plaut's boardinghouse, walked down the street and up the three steps of the white wooden porch.

Mrs. Plaut was just inside the screen door waiting for me, arms folded across her tiny twig of a body, clutching what looked like a tattered ream of paper to her slender bosom. Mrs. Plaut was somewhere between seventy-five and ninety, with the constitution of Primo Carnera and the energy of Ray Bolger. Her hearing had long ago begun to fail her, but she more than made up for it with eyesight and determination.

"Mr. Peelers, I have a list," she shouted.

"Mrs. Plaut," I answered loudly, seeing that she wasn't wearing her hearing aid. "This day has turned from a toe-tapping joy to thoughts, if not of suicide, at least of a dark room, a few hours of radio, and lots of dreamless sleep."

"Sometimes I fail to understand you, Mr. Peelers," she said with a shake of her head. "If your toes are cramped, don't climb in bed feeling sorry for yourself. Do what the Mister always did, stomp around the floor barefoot. And don't breathe in that Flit stuff."

Mrs. Plaut, when it fit her agenda, thought I was an exterminator or an editor for a small but prestigious publisher. I do not know where she got these ideas. Attempts to find out had proved both fruitless and maddening.

"I'll stomp around, Mrs. Plaut," I said.

"There is a potato shortage, you know," she said moving from small talk to Item One on her agenda.

"I've heard."

"There is a black market in potatoes."

"Ah," I said knowingly, looking longingly at the stairs behind her that led to my room.

"I should like you to use your resources to obtain as many pounds of baking potatoes as you can."

"Tomorrow," I said. "I'll think about it tomorrow. I promise."

"Promises are daisies. Delivering the goods is orchids. The Mister said that."

The Mister was long, long gone. I had never had the pleasure of meeting him. But he was a legend in the House of Plaut.

"And," she went on, "more meat rationing is coming April eleventh."

"I'll give you my meat-ration stamps," I said. "Now, if I can . . ."

She handed me the papers in her hand, lined sheets covered with Mrs. Plaut's precisely written pen-and-ink words. It was the latest chapter in the endless saga of her family. I was expected to edit—minimally—and comment—favorably—on each chapter handed to me. I was expected to do this quickly and to be ready for an interrogation to prove I had read her latest offering carefully.

"At breakfast tomorrow morning, you can critique," she said. "We're having Waterbury crescent scones crafted with mince, orange peel, and a dash of nutmeg."

"I'll have to make it a quick breakfast, Mrs. P.," I said, trying to inch past her, letting my slightly outstretched arms clutching her manuscript run interference.

But Mrs. Plaut was not to be denied. She cut me off.

"Where is it you have to run? Call, make it later. You have the chapter about Aunt Bess and Cousin Leo's fateful encounter with Pancho Villa."

"I have a dance lesson with Fred Astaire," I countered.

"The movie Fred Astaire?"

"Not the streetcar conductor," I said.

"He is trying to teach you to dance?"

"Yes," I said. "That's why I'm having a lesson."

"He will fail miserably," she said with a shake of her head.

"I appreciate your confidence and support," I said. "I'll read this tonight."

"Potatoes," she said, finally standing aside to let me pass.

I paused on the steps and turned to her with, "Have you ever seen Preston Stewart?"

"In the flesh, no. In the movies, yes."

"What do you think?"

"About Preston Stewart? If I were fifty years younger, I'd hide in his bedroom closet and jump on his bones when he came home."

"Thanks," I said, starting up the stairs. Behind me Mrs. Plaut said, "That's what my niece Rhoda did with Valentino. And she said it worked."

The only person I could or would talk to about me and Anne was Gunther Wherthman, who was my best friend, Swiss, and about the same size as Johnny Puleo of the Harmonica Rascals. He was either a midget or a little person, depending on who you were talking to. I wanted to talk to Gunther, who had gotten me the room in Mrs. Plaut's boardinghouse three years earlier when Mrs. Eastwood had thrown me out of my apartment. Gunther was always proper. Gunther was always perfectly dressed, down to his tiny three-piece suits and a fob with a regular-size watch attached. Gunther spent his days translating books into English from about a dozen languages. He had more work than he could handle with government contracts, industrial and popular publishers. But Gunther was out of town with the normal-sized young woman he was dating and considering marrying, a graduate student in music history at the University of San Francisco.

I didn't want to think about anybody marrying anybody.

I went into my room and was greeted by a loud series of demanding "meows" from Dash. The sun was almost down but not quite. I hit the light switch and surveyed my domicile, Mrs. Plaut's manuscript pages in my hand.

A flowery ancient sofa to my left had a purple pillow resting on it. Stitched onto the pillow by Mrs. Plaut was "God Bless Us Every One." There had been a bed, but since I didn't use it I finally convinced Mrs. Plaut that the room was too crowded and the frame and spring should be stored in the vast and overflowing garage in back of the house. The garage used to be a barn and still had the smell of long-ago livestock.

My bad back was a gift from a large Negro gentleman who had wanted to approach Mickey Rooney at a premiere. It had been my job to protect the Mick from overeager fans. I was all that stood between Rooney and the large gentleman. Rooney didn't even know what was going on. The big man had given me a bear hug and dropped me on the ground amid the crowd of fans. By then Rooney was safely inside his car and on his way. I, on the other hand, was crawling for open air and feeling a pain in my back that would haunt me on and off from then on.

I slept on a thin, hard mattress on the floor. I cleaned my room every morning and made the bed. Mrs. Plaut had frequent and unannounced inspections. The rooms of her boardinghouse had no locks, not even in the shared bathroom. Mrs. Plaut didn't believe in privacy. People only did things they shouldn't when they knew they could lock their doors.

I moved to the small table near the window to my right. The table had two chairs. There was a small refrigerator and a small built-in cupboard behind the table. Mrs. Plaut forbade stoves in the room, but we could have hot plates. One of her relatives, an uncle, I think, had been burned to death in his house on the Nebraska plains. It wasn't clear from her memoirs whether the deed had been done by Indians, bandits, or her aunt.

I got two cans of tuna from the shelf, opened them, gave Dash some fresh water and one can while I ate the other. I had a glass of milk and a couple of graham crackers decently dunked, took off my clothes and got under the blanket on my mattress, ill-prepared to deal with Mrs. Plaut's Aunt Rhoda, Cousin Leo, and Pancho Villa. Dash and whatever gods may be are my witnesses that I tried.

As soon as Pancho Villa appeared on page 1,122, my imagination cast Preston Stewart in the role. I couldn't shake the mental picture of all those teeth beneath the sombrero. I put the manuscript down and fell asleep to the sound of Dash lapping his water, planning a night on the neighborhood through the open window.

Chapter Three

I Won't Dance

On the way to Fred Astaire at R.K.O. on a Wednesday morning with a tankful of gas, and close to rich with four hundred dollars, I wondered about where I was going to get black-market potatoes for Mrs. Plaut and whether Preston Stewart and the former Anne Peters had spent all or part of the night together.

I drove, ignoring a small, strange clinking somewhere under the hood of the car. I listened to the radio. A cute voice urged, "Gimme a little kiss, will you, huh?"

I turned off the radio and thought about Arthur Forbes, Luna Martin, Fred Astaire, and my city.

In the twenties, with his honor Mayor George Cryer, who looked a little like Woodrow Wilson, presiding, there had been a boom, probably like no boom in American history.

In the twenties, Fred and his sister, Adele Astaire, were running across a stage in Los Angeles and waving their arms in the air. The audience loved it.

In the twenties, the University of California at Los Angeles sprang sprawling from the earth of Westwood. The Mulholland Highway was built. City Hall rose white and curious downtown. People moved in, speculated. Bought a house in the morning. Sold it at a profit that night. People had money and smiles on their faces. More than once at Beneva's Pharmacy, half a block down from my dad's grocery, I'd watched Mr. Pope line up the Coca-Colas on the counter for a group of real-estate salesmen. Then, one by one, he'd drop a five-grain Benzedrine tablet in their drink to, as Mr. Pope said, "perk 'em up and keep 'em on the happiness track."

Fred and Adele were touring the country, with Fred singing "Fascinating Rhythm" and dancing to "S'Wonderful."

In the twenties, there was money to be made and laws to be broken. Jazz and Prohibition hit Los Angeles. Bookmakers, gamblers, and prostitutes set up shop and handed out cards. Morality laws, alcohol laws, gangs moving in. Even in Glendale, where I was a kid cop, there were opportunities on the street to earn enough fast money to buy a house and make your wife happy. I had two partners when I was on the force. Both were on the take. Both thought they had good reasons. I was young and had a brother on the Los Angeles Police Department who would break your fingers if you tried to slip him green paper. But there weren't many Phil Pevsners on the police force. It was a golden opportunity for Fingers Intaglia to change his name and come to the boom town as the official representative of Detroit's Purple Gang and the son-in-law of Guiseppi Cortona.

In the twenties, Fred Astaire, wearing a striped beret and matching socks, was back on Broadway playing the accordion, leaping to "New Sun in the Sky," and doing a dream ballet to "The Beggar's Waltz." The papers said he had bought a $22,000 Rolls Royce which he never drove.

Police captains grew rich; patrolmen and detectives didn't do badly either. In 1923, in an attempt to purge the police department, the city of Los Angeles hired August Vollmer, then chief at Berkeley and hailed as the incorruptible father of modern police science, to head the department, clean it up. He had one year to do it. He started the Los Angeles Police Department school, and one of its first graduates was James Edgar "Two Gun" Davis, who two years later became L.A. Police Chief, followed by Roy "Strong Arm Dick" Steckel. There were raids in 1923, lots of them, but the big-buck bad guys had taken a one-year vacation, leaving the small operators—who had to keep making a living—to get their wares busted and one-way tickets out of town or into prison. Success for Vollmer, and then his term came to an end in September 1924. Just before his one-year term ended, billboards began springing up, reading, "The First of September will be the Last of August." And it was. Things were back to normal, and people like Arthur Forbes, the former Fingers Intaglia, simply raised their prices and doubled their payoffs, and took over the operations of the smaller gangsters who were behind bars or back in Dayton or Troy terrorizing the locals. Arthur Forbes bought buildings and people and land and more cops.

Those with dollars in their pockets and those with no dollars, to work for those with dollars. The Mexican border was wide open.

Then the Depression hit. Latins, even if they were American citizens, were rounded up, herded on trains, shipped over the border, and told they would be jailed or shot if they returned. Illegal border checks, the bum's brigade, were set up on the major highways and roads. And if the cop on the border didn't like your face or your wife's or the amount of money in your pocket, he could turn you back. Chinatown was shut down and leveled after a vigorous campaign by Harry Chandler, publisher of the *Los Angeles Times*. The Chinese scattered, most of them going east, reverse Oriental Oakies. Union Station went up in their place, and in 1938 a new, much smaller seven-acre tourist attraction called China

City went up fast, giving jobs to voters, none of whom were Chinese. You could get a phony rickshaw ride around China City for a quarter. A year after it opened, China City mysteriously burned down to the ground, putting the remaining Chinese who had become tourist attractions out of work.

But now we had Fred Astaire on the screen in the dark, smiling, dancing, *Flying Down to Rio*, singing, getting Ginger. He looked like one of us. He could dance as if he had found a way to defeat gravity and fatigue. And nothing bothered him. Getting off a train with Victor Moore, walking down the street in a tux with empty pockets, Fred could always see the bright side.

In L.A., the Arthur Forbeses were grabbing more land cheap and keeping whole precincts happy. People were hungry. There were lines at Clifton's Cafeterias, the cafeterias of the golden rule, where all you had to do was refuse to pay your bill for any reason and you wouldn't be charged.

And Fred Astaire tilted his little sailor cap over his right eye, hitched up his bell-bottom trousers, and danced around the deck of an R.K.O. battleship, telling us it was okay to "put all our eggs in one basket."

What mattered was a job, any job. The county started to build sewers and highways, using federal and state funds and bonds bought generously by the people who still had money, people like Arthur Forbes who legally began to buy the city. But people were working. Working the sewer detail in a gas mask for the Los Angeles Department of Public Works was a great opportunity.

And Fred in a suit and tie and a pair of brown-and-white shoes leaped over a low railing onto a dance floor, took Ginger's hand, started his feet tapping, and advised us with a smile to "Let Yourself Go."

And there were disasters. Major floods in 1934 and 1938 from sudden ten-inch downpours that lasted only a few hours. The Los Angeles River went over its banks, driving people from their houses in a wild search for anything that would float. A major earthquake struck around Long Beach and Compton. And fires. Mostly fires. In 1938 the Baker Block, built in the 1870's, a major tourist attraction, was hit hard by fire.

And Fred in elegant tie and tails, arms floating to the music like a magician, said, "The hell with it. Hum 'The Picolino,' dance 'The Carioca' and 'The Continental.' "

When I got to the gate at R.K.O., a guy in a gray uniform, complete with black-leather strap over his shoulder and matching cap fixed evenly down to his eyebrows, walked out of the guard booth and motioned for me to roll down the window. The look on his well-shaved face made it clear that he didn't like leaning down so far and he didn't much understand who would be trying to get through the R.K.O. gate in a battered refrigerator on wheels.

"Yes, sir?" he said, but I somehow felt that the "sir" had a professional tinge of contempt.

"Name's Peters, Toby Peters. I have an appointment with Fred Astaire."

The guard nodded. His body and head squared, face flat and gray, the smell of retired cop on his Sen-Sen breath.

"Astaire's gonna teach me to dance," I explained.

The guard looked at me and nodded. A pro. No expression, just a brief blink of the eyes.

"I'll check," he said. "Meanwhile, please just sit where you are."

Since my only option, now that there was another car behind me, was to crash through the gate, I sat. The clink under the hood had grown worse. The seat next to me smelled like cat and I sat inside wearing some reasonably clean trousers, a tieless white shirt that I had tried, with some success, to flatten out with Gunther's iron.

The guard lumbered to the gate house and made a call as he watched me through the window. In my rearview mirror I could see Butterfly McQueen in a blue Buick, watching me with impatience. I shrugged. The guard came back.

"Stage Two," he said. "You just . . ."

"I know how to get there," I said. "I did a few security jobs. That was a while ago, but I think I can find my way."

"You were in the agency business and now you're a dancer?" the guard said, brow furrowed.

"Life can be strange and wondrous," I said.

"It can also be shit," he whispered.

Butterfly McQueen hit her horn, and the guard pulled his head out of my window and waved me on.

I parked right next to the entrance to Stage Two between two piles of light stands and thick coiled wires. The on-stage light was out so I went in. I went through a bank of floor-to-ceiling dark curtains and came out on a black polished floor covered with footprints and scuff marks. Fred Astaire sat alone at a table in one corner. There was no furniture on the stage except for the large table on which sat a phonograph, a stack of records, and lunch. Astaire had a soup spoon in his hand. Another place was set across the table.

"Toby, I'm glad you came," he said, rising and taking my hand. "I was afraid you'd changed your mind. Arthur Forbes . . ."

Astaire was dressed in white slacks, a dark-blue, long-sleeved billowy shirt, and a small white scarf tied around his neck.

"Shall we dance?" I said.

He smiled and waved toward the table.

"Shall we eat first? I took the liberty of ordering. I don't like eating in the commissary. I hope you haven't had an early lunch?"

"Nope," I said as he took his seat and I joined him.

"Chicken noodle soup," Astaire said as I picked up my spoon. "The trick is in the noodles. The noodles must be wide and flat. I'm afraid the ice cream is starting to melt a little."

"Looks fine," I said, reaching for a bottle of Ruppert Beer near my soup. I opened it with a shining church key conveniently placed in front of my bowl and poured the beer into a tall glass. I drank the beer and tasted the soup.

"How do you like it?" Astaire said with a real interest.

"Flat noodles," I said, holding up a spoonful.

"That's the secret," he confirmed solemnly.

I gave him the very short version of my background as we finished eating. He nodded, listened, asked a question about my brother, Phil, and what I thought of various people I'd worked with, for, and, once in a while, against.

"You ever run into Preston Stewart?" I asked.

"Preston . . ." he nibbled his lower lip, looked down at the table, and then snapped his fingers. "Right. Tall, tennis-player tan. B pictures."

"That's the one."

"Ran into him a few times," said Astaire. "Not much conversation, but he seemed likable enough and, as I remember, he was remarkably informed about dance."

"I'm ready," I said, getting up.

Astaire rose, turned a knob to warm up the phonograph, and stepped out onto the scuffed, massive floor.

"I'm going to walk you through some basic steps," he said. "I'll keep it simple. Stop me if you don't understand. When you give Luna Martin the lesson, just do what I'm doing."

I nodded.

"Good," he said, rubbing his hands. "Very good. Now I'll just put on a record."

The record he put on was ancient and scratched, but I recognized "Hindustan" and would have bet that it was Isham Jones.

"Now," said Astaire, "do this. Two sliding steps forward and one short one to your left."

He demonstrated. I mimicked.

"Not bad," he said. "Now do the same thing to the music. Pick up the beat and you'll be doing the fox-trot."

"We have a problem," I said.

"You have a wooden leg," Astaire said over the steady sound of the music.

"No," I said.

"You are going blind. You suffer from horrible vertigo when you dance. You are massively embarrassed and have what you hope is a temporary insane feeling that you can't move."

"None of the above," I said. "I can't hear a beat."

"Even the deaf can hear the beat, feel its vibration," said Astaire. "Try it."

I tried.

"Listen," he said. "I'll say 'beat, beat, beat, beat,' and you put your left foot out on the beat."

"Right," I said.

When that didn't work, he tried counting one-two-three-four.

Ten minutes and three records later I still hadn't found the beat. I hadn't heard it. I decided it was some mysterious thing that other people heard and I was cursed to never experience.

Astaire was rubbing his chin and watching my feet. "You are a challenge," he said.

I shrugged.

"We'll search for the beat until you find it," he said. "This time, forget the music. Just listen for the beat. The music will take care of itself."

We searched for ten minutes more when Astaire finally said, "Stop."

I stopped. We had been trying to find the beat in a waltz. I had been given to understand that there were three.

"I suggest that if Miss Martin asks you to show her a step, turn off the music, claim a case of dancer's arthritis, and walk through the step. There will be a mercifully small number of steps to go through."

He showed me steps. Tango, swing, fox-trot, waltz. I drew little pictures in my notebook with comments like, "Hesitation step, follow the flow of dance, keep your arms up, don't dance on your heels, and don't look at your partner when you're waltzing or doing the fox-trot."

After almost two hours of this, Astaire said, "Enough" and took off a Sammy Kaye recording of "Brown Eyes."

He stood at the table in silence, looking at me, tapping his slender fingers together.

"It won't work," he said. "I thought I could teach anyone, but . . ."

"I can fake it," I said. "It's part of my job."

"I'm beginning to think this is not a terribly good idea," Astaire said, plunging his hands into his pockets and heading toward me.

"I'm a professional," I reminded him.

"So is Arthur Forbes," he said.

"We have a deal," I reminded him. "But if you want your money back . . ." I reached for my wallet. He held out his left hand to stop me.

"Go ahead," he said with a sigh. "But be careful."

"If 'careful' works," I said.

"All right," Astaire said, arms folded, tapping his fingers on his elbows. "Once more."

We concentrated on the waltz. I led him around the floor and before I flattened too many of his toes, he said, "Okay, forget the beat. Confidence. Complete confidence and a smile. Back straight. Stomach in. Elbows up. Use the whole floor. It's yours."

Something came over me when I didn't have to worry about the beat. The "Missouri Waltz" scratched away on the phonograph and something inside me said, "What the hell." I danced. I flowed. I led. I made my boxes, did progressives, turned Astaire. And then the music stopped.

"Not bad," he said.

I was trying to catch my breath. I leaned over.

"I don't know what I did," I said.

"That, I could tell," said Astaire. "But you pretended. You got carried away. Confidence will take you across any ballroom."

"Hearing the beat would also help."

"By pure luck you'll get it about a quarter of the time," Astaire said.

"I guess I'll have to count on pure luck," I said, straightening up.

"See this floor?" he said, looking down. "When we dance on a floor like this, we have to keep stopping so a crew can come in and clean up the foot marks. They all show on film. So you dance your routine and stop and wait while the ground crew comes in on their hands and knees with buckets and towels."

There was a moral here but I wasn't getting it.

"You are polishing my floor. I am sitting around waiting. You have the dirty job. I dance."

"I also get paid," I reminded him.

"So do I," he said. "Which makes it much easier to watch young men endlessly polish the floor. Good luck, Toby. You have my number. Call me at home."

We shook hands and he escorted me to the stage door.

"I think I'll stay here for a while," he said. "A few steps I want to try. Besides, I want to be sure I can still find the beat."

The next day was Thursday, the day I met Luna Martin, Fingers Intaglia, and the Beast of Bombay, whose hand print was probably indelibly welted to my ass. Driving Lou Canton back to Glendale in agony and listening to him complain didn't help my disposition.

I spent most of the rest of the day finding backup. I'd been told gently by Jeremy's wife, Alice, that I was not to call on him for help again. Or, as she put it in a calming voice as we stood on the stairway of the Farraday Building while she gently rocked Baby Natasha, "If you so much as suggest that you might need his help for one of your dangerous, silly cases, I'll personally tear off three of your toes."

It was an effective warning. Alice, at nearly three hundred pounds, could do the job. But what made it effective was the specific number, *three,* the choice of an inspired imagination or someone who had thought long and hard about what might be effectively said and done.

Gunther Wherthman was my second choice. Tiny, easy to spot, maybe, but smart and loyal. Except Gunther was up north. That left Shelly, a less than formidable body, but a body.

I stopped at a diner called Mack's on Melrose, ordered a tuna on white toast with a pickle and fries from an ancient waitress in a uniform left over from the Dr. Kildare series. Near the cash register was a display of emergency first-aid supplies—aspirin, Band-aids, Ex-Lax, and an ugly-looking pain salve in a purple jar. I picked up the jar. Then I called the office.

Violet answered, "Dr. Sheldon Minck's office."

"This is the office of Minck and Peters," I corrected. "Can I help you?"

"Is this a joke?" she asked.

"Mrs. Gonsenelli, this is Mr. Peters. I thought we agreed that you would answer the phone with 'Minck and Peters, can I help you?' "

"Dr. Minck changed that," she said. "He says he pays the phone bill and you should . . ."

"Put him on," I said.

"He's with a patient."

"Let the patient bleed to death," I said pleasantly. "It'll be more humane than what Shelly must be putting him through."

"I'll tell him," she said, and the phone clicked against the top of her little table.

I imagined her drawing up tight and wedging through the thin space between the desk and wall. Voices and then, "I've got a patient, Toby," he said. "A new thing I'm trying. Killing the nerves. I've got to get back to him."

Beyond and behind Shelly came the moan of the *Lusitania* as it finally sank into the Atlantic.

"Minck and Peters," I said.

"It's not good for business."

"Yours or mine?"

"Mine," he said. "You should have your own line."

"Hard to get with a war on."

"Then you pay half the phone bill," he said, obviously playing to the alert Violet Gonsenelli.

"It's built into my rent."

"Built into . . . who said that? When? How? Why? You make things up. I'm a victim here."

More moans from the patient beneath the sea.

"One dollar a month more," I said.

"One dollar? You must be . . ."

". . . making my final offer," I said.

"One dollar," Shelly agreed.

"Don't hang up. I may need your help, Shel."

"Help?"

"I may need some people to protect a client."

"Astaire?"

"Yes."

"Fred Astaire? You want me to become a private investigator for a while and protect Fred Astaire?"

"Did Violet catch all of that? Is she impressed?"

"I think so," said Shelly as his patient let out an "agggggghhhhhh." "I don't care if it's dangerous. When do you need me?"

"Nine tomorrow morning," I said. "Ballroom of the Monticello Hotel on Sunset."

"I'll cancel my morning patients. Should I bring my gun?"

"You don't have a gun, Shel."

"I understand," Sheldon said seriously. "I'll be there. Violet wants to talk to you."

He handed her the phone and walked away, calling to the moaning patient, "Jesus Christ, can't you take a little pain without acting like a baby?"

"Mr. Peters?"

"Yes, Violet."

"Jimmy Bivins is five-to-six to beat Tami Mauriello Friday. I'll take Bivins and give you four-to-six on six dollars with an extra two dollars that say the fight goes the distance."

"Our Ortiz-Salica bet still on?"

"I've got Ortiz, two dollars."

"You're on on the Bivins fight," I said and hung up.

I lined up Pook Hurawitz and Jerry Rogasinian, both bit actors and part-time stunt men who could be counted on for a good show if you paid them. They both looked like what they frequently played, gangsters who helped fill out the gang and never uttered a word. I was type-casting them.

Pook asked who we were working for. He upped his price to twenty bucks a day from the fifteen I offered him. I could have gotten Rogasinian for fifteen but I was sure they'd talk about what I was paying them so I just offered the twenty. Jerry was grateful.

"Jerry, you ever work on a film with Preston Stewart?" I asked after we had agreed to terms.

"Twice," he said. "On *Hell in Himalaya* I was one of the Sherpa carriers. And on *Night of Destiny* I played a cab driver. Had one word. Preston comes to me on the curb and says, 'You free?' and I answered, 'Sure.'"

"What's Preston Stewart like?"

"Good guy," Jerry said. "No star crap. Drank coffee with the rest of us. Joked around. Polite to the women. Good guy. Why?"

"I think he's going to marry my ex-wife."

"I take it back," Jerry said. "Stewart was an asshole."

"Too late, Jerry. I'll see you tomorrow."

I hung up the phone and went back to the counter to eat my sandwich and drink a Pepsi.

"Toast is cold," the waitress said, hands on hips, challenging me to blame her or deny it. "Why don't you sit down?"

"Cold toast is fine," I said. "Can't sit. I was spanked by a giant from India."

"Want me to do it again?"

"Nope. I'm in enough pain already."

"No," she said. "I meant, do you want me to give you fresh toast?"

"I'm all right. I could use a little ketchup."

She nodded. "You're Tobias Pevsner, aren't you?" she said, handing me the bottle of Heinz.

"Right," I said, pouring ketchup and looking a little more closely at her.

A distant aunt? A former client? She sagged under an oversized white starched uniform; tight curls of white hair crept out from under her Nurse Duncan cap. Her skin was pale and her lips colorless.

"Anita Maloney," she said.

"Anita?"

"Tobias," she said. "You took me to the senior prom. You tried to get under my pink crinoline dress and into my cotton panties."

There was one other customer at the counter, a round man wearing a delivery cap. He had three folds of skin on the back of his neck. He ate slowly, mechanically, from a bowl that looked as if it contained the same swill that the Count of Monte Christo was forced to gulp down in the Chateau Des Ifs. He tried not to look at me and Anita. I forced myself to look at Anita. She was a year, maybe two years younger than me and she looked like someone's angry grandmother.

"Anita," I said, putting down my sandwich. "How the heck have you been? You look terrific."

"You look pretty much the same," she said, eyeing me. "A few more kicks in the face. A few more pounds. Eat your food before it gets too cold."

I ate and shook my head in an isn't-it-a-small-world shake.

"So . . ." I said with a mouthful of tuna, "how the heck have you been?"

"Life story fast?" she asked, leaning forward.

"Sure," I said.

"Married Ozzie Shaw. Remember him?"

"Football team, straight A's?"

"That's him," she said with a grin.

"How is he?"

"Dead," she said. "That's why I'm grinning and happy to be on my feet behind a counter hauling grease."

"I gather it was a less than happy union."

"Liar, womanizer, hitter, shiftless. And those were his good points."

I smiled, keeping my mouth shut as I chewed, and looked over at the man with the extra-thick neck. He was still shoveling.

"We had one kid, Lonny," she said. "Here."

She reached under her apron and came up with a pocket-sized cardboard folder. She took out a photograph and slid it forward next to the plate.

There was the Anita Maloney I knew. I didn't recognize Ozzie, who had his arm around her shoulder. The kid standing between them was maybe five or six.

"Cute," I said, sliding the photograph back. "Ozzie changed."

"That's not Ozzie," she said, putting the photograph back. "That's Charlie, Lonny's husband. He's in the army. Prisoner of war. Japs. The boy is my grandson, Mal."

"Great-looking kid," I said.

"That's not the end of my story," she said with a smile that suggested much more. "But we'll save that. What's your short-and-sweet tale? I heard you married Anne Mitzenmacher. How's your brother?"

"Anne and I were married and divorced, no kids," I said, dipping fries in ketchup and wondering how I'd escape. "And Phil's a captain with the L.A.P.D. Three kids."

"You still a cop? I heard you were a cop."

"Not for a long time," I said. "I'm a private investigator."

"Like Mike Shayne?"

"A little," I said, looking at my wristwatch.

"You got a card? I've got something you might help with."

I found a withered edged card in my wallet and handed it to Anita. She looked at it and put it into the pocket of her white uniform. There was no check and I didn't want to wait for one. I pulled out two bucks, plenty for the drink, sandwich, and salve, and the most generous tip Anita Maloney was likely to get in her entire career, at least from a sober customer.

"Generous," she said, picking up the bills and my plate.

"You know where I can get some potatoes?" I asked.

"Potatoes?"

"Five pounds."

Anita shrugged and disappeared into the kitchen. I exchanged looks with the eating machine. Anita was back almost instantly with a paper bag.

"This is about five pounds," she said, handing the bag to me. "Thirty cents."

"Thanks, Anita," I said, reaching into my pocket for change.

"You left more than enough," she said, holding up the two dollar bills. "Maybe we can get together some time and talk about Glendale," she said. "Here, I'll write down my phone number."

She pulled out a pencil and scribbled her name and number on a napkin and handed it to me.

"It'd be fun," I said, folding the napkin and stuffing it into my pocket.

"I clean up real good," she said.

"That makes one of us," I said over my shoulder, heading for the door. "Take care, Anita."

The eating man's stomach gurgled. He pulled out a red-and-white package of Twenty Grand cigarettes and looked around for matches.

Getting back into my Crosley was as close to hell as a human is likely to get. My rear end wept with electric bursts. I drove home trying not to think about the pain or about Anita Maloney. There had been a thirtieth reunion of my high-school class not long ago. I hadn't gone. I told myself I never had anything in common with my classmates and I hadn't liked Glendale High. I knew now that I didn't want to look at their faces, to see dopey Gregg Lean with no hair and a big belly, and Anita Maloney, without saying a word, telling me to go look in the mirror.

I was back at Mrs. Plaut's boardinghouse and halfway up the stairs when I heard behind me, "Mr. Peelers."

I turned with a smile, paper bag in hand.

"Mrs. Plaut."

"My manuscript."

"I'll finish it this afternoon. Here are the potatoes you wanted."

"Needed, not wanted," she said, meeting me halfway and taking the bag in her thin arms. She smelled the potatoes and, satisfied, looked up at me.

"I will go to my chambers now," she said, "and listen to Tommy Riggs and Betty Lou and Elmer Davis and 'The Week's War News.' By then I would think you will have finished my chapter."

"You are too generous, Mrs. P.," I said.

"Sarcasticisms?"

"I'm sorry," I said. "I've got a lot on my mind."

My voice must have dropped from the usual scream with which I normally addressed Mrs. Plaut because she answered with, "I can rewind my own clocks, thank you. I have since the Mister died, and I'll probably find a way to do it after I die."

"I'd bet on it," I said. "Mrs. Plaut. How old would you say I am?"

"How? . . ."

"Old."

"Young," she said. "Everybody looks young. You look maybe a little older than most. Sixty."

"I'm not even fifty," I said.

"Fifty, sixty, what's the difference," she said with a shrug, turning her back on me and heading down the stairs, potato booty in hand, humming "Glow Worm."

I headed to my room, pushed open the door, and went to my cupboard. Dash was sitting in the open window, ignoring me, fascinated by something in the yard.

"Hello to you too," I said, fixing myself a very generous bowl of Kix and milk even though I wasn't hungry. "Care to join me?"

Dash turned to look at me and the Kix and then turned back to the apparently fascinating show in the yard.

I ate cereal standing and read Mrs. Plaut's manuscript, page by page. It began:

> Aunt Bess had an uncommon fondness for Cousin Leo. Uncommon. They were not kin. Aunt Bess was married to Uncle Seymour who sold junk to Indians. He was very bad at selling junk to Indians. He got into the business too late. By the time he heard about it and moved West, the Indians had considerable experience in being sold junk. As it was, some of the Indians sold the junk they had bought from white men back to Uncle Seymour. Should you conclude by this that Uncle Seymour was not acute, you would be right. Uncle Seymour had a son by the name of Leo who had been born to Uncle Seymour's first wife, Hannah, who, it is reported, had a left eye that looked no place that much made sense. So, my mother's sister Bess who was no Disraeli but neither was she a fool washed her hands of Uncle Seymour and ran away to Mexico with

Cousin Leo who was pleasant to look at but not much higher of sense than Calvin Burkett who everyone knows is and will ever be an idiot boy. Uncle Seymour did not follow them. Instead, he took his junk wagon and headed to Texas where he was certain to find someone less acute than the Indians.

In Mexico, Aunt Bess and Cousin Leo built a cabin near Juarez with an eye toward raising corn and chickens and children. This in spite of the fact that Aunt Bess was a full fifty-five years of age and Cousin Leo someone in the vicinity of twenty. No one, not even his own father, knew for sure and apparently the age of Cousin Leo was of no interest to any member of the family until I began these researches.

It was then that Pancho Villa the dreaded bandit entered their peaceful though profitless lives. The bandit saw Aunt Bess in the market bargaining for tripe and was immediately enamored of her. Aunt Bess had a pleasant face and large body parts.

The dreaded bandit kidnapped Aunt Bess from the market and he rode away with her dragging tripe and screaming, "I am being kidnapped by the dreaded bandit Pancho Villa." Now since everyone could plainly see this including Cousin Leo who stood watching there was little to comment on at the moment, though Cousin Leo later reported that a woman said in English for his benefit that Pancho Villa was known to have the taste of a snout hog. Three days later Aunt Bess had not returned to the village so Cousin Leo, whose Spanish was on the minimum and lacking in refinement, donned a hat of *ala ancha* (which means wide brimmed), sold what he was able of the small farm including the chickens and the house and set off in search of his paramour.

It was at this juncture that Cousin Leo's story strains

even family good will. In his travel which took him to a mountain village where Pancho Villa was reported to be staying Cousin Leo in search of someone who could speak English wandered into a drinking establishment which in Mexico is called a cantina or at least was when Cousin Leo chanced into one. There at a table dealing cards in a game of poker was a painted woman of uncertain age with a wild left eye.

Mother? Leo inquired and sure enough the woman dealing poker in that cantina was his mother Hannah. There is no report from Leo—his story having been told to me by his daughter, also Hannah—that mother and son embraced. After the hand of cards was dealt Hannah did inquire of Uncle Seymour and learned the story of her son and her husband's second wife. Since Hannah's Spanish and connections in the town were more than adequate and she was up for something like adventure after having dealt poker for more than ten years she and Leo set forth in search of Aunt Bess. In the mountains they came upon a quartet of banditos who claimed they were in the army of the dreaded Villa. They had a powwow on whether to ravish Hannah and dispatch Leo but Hannah's Spanish and advanced age saved the day. She claimed to have some information of military import for Villa's ears only.

To make a long story a short story they were led into the presence of Villa his own self. Villa, a portly man of no great beauty, was seated upon a rock sucking out the marrow of what appeared to be the bone of a goat. Though his view of the dreaded bandit had been but fleeting Cousin Leo was as certain as his poor mind would allow that this was not the man who had taken Aunt Bess. As it turned out he was correct. It had been an underling of Villa who had taken Bess. Oh the ignominy.

Villa readily agreed to exchange Aunt Bess for Hannah which suited Hannah though she knew the adventure would be short lived. Bess was returned to Leo but the union did not last. She abandoned him in Puerto Del Sol claiming she had forgotten her comb and had to go back to the Villa camp to recover it.

Cousin Leo sat in the town square of Puerto Del Sol for seven days exhausting his money and the patience of the town folk and singing various hymns particularly "Rock of Ages" to pass the time. He was driven out by stick and stone, running down the road with one hand upon his wide brimmed hat to keep from losing it and screaming as he ran, "Life is too much work for a simple man." Cousin Leo found himself in Stickney, California, married a woman named Leona who was if the story is to be believed for I have never met her of even less wit than Cousin Leo, who opened a hat shop and made a living.

Aunt Bess and Aunt Hannah emerged in Mexico City some months after Leo's departure and running as the Gringa Sisters were elected to the newly formed Godless government of Mexico.

There is more. Oh time triumphant! Would that I endure to tell the whole of my tale.

I laid the pages of Mrs. Plaut's manuscript flat on my small table, looked to Dash for support and guidance, and went to the phone in the hall to call Carmen, the cashier at Levy's. I invited her to a movie. I told her that I was in pain and needed a gentle hand to cover my sore spots with salve. She said her son had chicken pox. Mrs. Plaut wasn't around so I left the manuscript in front of her door with a note saying, "Brilliant work. The plight of Cousin Leo particularly touched me. Villa was a cad."

I walked downtown carrying a pillow under my arm and a look on my homely face that challenged anyone to ask me why I was carrying a pillow. It wasn't more than a mile, and walking was better than trying to get back in the Crosley. I went to the movies by myself, sat on the pillow, and saw *Across the Pacific*, with Bogart and Mary Astor. The newsreel told me that the Office of War Information had asked deferments for Kay Kayser, Edgar Bergen, Red Skelton, Bob Hope, Nelson Eddy, Freeman Gosden, and Lanny Ross so they could contribute to the war effort by entertaining the troops. I couldn't keep sitting so I got up and watched most of the show from the back of the theater, leaning against the wall. The manager, who recognized me as a more-or-less regular, came over to ask me in a whisper if there was something wrong with the seats.

"War wound acting up," I said.

"I've still got a piece of metal shaped like a small fish in my back from the Marne," he said sympathetically.

I picked up a couple of hot dogs at The Pup and brought them home to share with Dash. Mrs. Plaut hadn't touched the manuscript that still lay in front of her door. I went to my room, gave Dash a dog without the bun, dropped my pants and underwear carefully, and did my best to swab the salve on my behind. At first it hurt. It stung. It cried. It made me wish I could say something in Indian that even Gunther might now know but that would be the major verbal attack in the long and violent life of Kudlap Singh, the Beast of Bombay. I danced around the room for a few minutes and it began to feel better. In about five minutes, I felt well enough to get stomach-down on my mattress to listen to Milton Berle and "We, the People." Mrs. Lou Gehrig was the guest.

Then I listened to "Amos and Andy." Kingfish was taking

it easy at home when his wife, Sapphire, came in and complained about the Kingfish not earning a living. She threatened to leave him unless he found a way to buy a car. Kingfish and Andy joined forces to make the investment. Before they got six blocks from the dealer in their 1926 Overland Roadster, the car broke down and they opened the trunk. There Andy and Kingfish found a body. Lawyer Algonquin J. Calhoun told them to sell the car. They tried to stick Shorty the barber with it, but he couldn't drive. Eventually, they discovered that the body was a mannequin. The boys had escaped the electric chair.

The world was right again.

I went to bed early and slept badly. Because of my bad back, I'm not supposed to sleep on my stomach, but I had no choice. Sometime in the night I got up, staggered to the bathroom in the hall, bare-assed and not caring even though Mrs. Plaut had one female roomer, Miss Reynal, a pretty enough woman, a little younger than myself but too skinny to rouse my interest. I wiped the salve off my throbbing behind, made it back to my room unseen, placed a pillow beneath me, and eased myself onto it, facing the ceiling. Not good, but better than the alternative.

I slept and dreamed of my senior prom. Everyone there was a kid but me. I was the same me I saw in the mirror every morning. I didn't belong at a senior prom with Anita Maloney, who looked the same as she had on that warm May night thirty years ago. Everyone was looking at me, everyone but Anne, who was a girl again and dancing with Koko the Clown, who gave me a big, lecherous open-mouthed grin and a wink.

I woke up with Dash sleeping on my chest, my tongue twice its normal size, and my behind still screaming.

The next day, Friday, I took the pillow from my sofa, the one that had "God Bless Us Every One" sewn in red on it, placed it on the seat of my Crosley, and found that I could drive with less discomfort than I had the day before. With Shelly, Pook Hurawitz, and Jerry Rogasinian as backup, I returned to the Monticello Hotel for a final try at convincing Luna Martin that Fred Astaire wasn't coming, not ever.

As it turned out, it wasn't necessary to convince her.

Chapter Four

Dancing on the Ceiling

I stood in the middle of the finely polished white floor and placed Pook behind me on the left and Jerry on the right, after paying them both up front and assuring them that there was no danger.

While we waited, Jerry reminded me that he had been trained in Shakespeare in Fort Worth, and I was suitably impressed. Pook said he had an audition in Culver City for a Roy Rogers movie at one.

Lou Canton shuffled in a few minutes after us, carrying a small metal toolbox in one hand and a folder of sheet music under the other arm.

"Lou," I said. "I told you I'd call if I needed you."

Lou continued toward the bandstand.

"You said today. I'm here today. You pay today."

He began setting up and I decided to deal with Lou later.

Another five minutes and Shelly showed up. "Sorry I'm late," he said, adjusting his glasses and stumbling toward me.

He was wearing denim pants, a blue work shirt, and a brown leather flight jacket that was at least a size too small for him. It was Shelly's tough-guy attitude. When he was close enough to see Pook and Jerry, Shelly stopped cold.

"Are these? . . ." he whispered to me so that his voice echoed through the room.

"No, this is Pook and Jerry. They're with us."

Jerry shook his head in disbelief. Pook gave me a what's-he-playing-comic-relief? look.

"Shelly's the perfect decoy," I said to Pook and Jerry. "They see us and we're just what they expected. They see Shelly and they get scared. He must be something special. Nothing else explains his being with us."

"Thanks, Toby. Great teeth," Shelly said, admiring the actors. "Who're we? . . ."

"Woman named Luna Martin and a man named Arthur Forbes," I said, watching the doors. "Stand over there, Shel."

I pointed in the general direction of the bandstand, where Lou had the top of the piano open again. "They didn't fix it," he groaned. "How can I play on this? You want rinky-dinky ragtime, I'll give it, but forget quality here." He stood up, toolbox in his hands, and headed for the door. "I'll be back," he said. "I'll fix it myself and charge you."

I didn't try to stop him.

Shelly set himself up in front of the bandstand and turned, looking out at us with his best scowl. He pulled a fresh cigar from his jacket pocket and put it into the corner of his mouth. He was doing his Al Capone, but it was coming out as a nearsighted Lou Costello. Then it hit him.

"Arthur For—Fingers Intaglia? The one who cut Stew Edelstein's fingers off and fed them to his German shepherds?"

"He wasn't convicted," I said. "Wasn't even charged for that."

"Because Stew put his hands through the opening of his steering wheel, started the car with his teeth, and headed for Key West," Shelly said, looking at Jerry and Pook, his face in putty panic.

From the hallway beyond the closed doors, we suddenly heard the sounds of an argument—a woman's shrill voice, but no words.

I looked at Pook and Jerry. They were character actors, but not in Thomas Mitchell's salary category. They were looking scared and starting to wonder if they both had immediate auditions at Republic.

"Toby," Pook said after exchanging a meaningful look with Jerry. "You didn't tell us . . ."

"Look," Shelly broke in, stepping off the bandstand. "I just recalled. I've got a patient waiting . . ."

It was then that the double doors of the ballroom flew open and Luna Martin in white silk dress swept in, her hair wild, her eyes wide, her breasts heaving. She looked at us and came straight for me, swaying, heels clacking—showing me, I thought, that she had indeed learned the fox-trot. I didn't notice the blood on her neck till she stood before us, held out both hands, and melted to the floor, her dress clinging, her hair billowing out on the marble. It was an entrance worthy of applause but nobody clapped. I moved to Luna's side.

"Who did this?" I asked, kneeling.

She looked up at me, pointed at Shelly, and closed her eyes forever.

"Hey," said Shelly, hurrying toward us, "I didn't kill her. Never saw her before this second."

"She dead?" asked Jerry, moving toward me.

I nodded.

"A looker," said Jerry.

"Let's get the hell out of here," Pook said, holding up two hands palm-down to keep the situation calm.

"Maybe I looked like someone else to her," Shelly pleaded.

"Nobody else looks like you, Shel," I said.

I got up and was about to tell them that we didn't have

much choice, that we'd have to call the police. Pook took a couple of steps toward the kitchen door. It opened and Kudlap Singh filled the doorway. Our eyes met. I automatically put both hands on my *tuchis*. I looked toward the double doors through which Luna had staggered. Arthur Forbes stood there, looking first at me and then at the fallen Luna. His face showed nothing as he walked slowly forward, glared at me for an instant, and glanced down at Luna.

"She's dead," I said.

"That I can see," Forbes said. "I know a dead person when I see one."

His face didn't change, but his eyes were moist. He knelt at Luna's side and touched her hair and her cheek, let out a deep sigh, and stood facing me.

"You are dead," he said, waving his arm in a gesture that took in me, Jerry, and Pook.

"We didn't kill her, Forbes," I said. "She walked in and fell right there a few seconds before you walked in."

"I said," Forbes repeated. "You are dead."

"Hey," said Pook, stepping forward. "We're just actors. Peters hired us to come in and play tough guys."

"That's right," said Jerry. "Did you see *May Time*? I was one of the Indians."

"Right," said Pook. "And when she came in she said the fat guy killed her."

He nodded at Shelly.

"He's right," Jerry agreed.

Shelly was too scared to speak, but his glasses were starting to slip down his nose the way they did when he had a particularly reluctant tooth in his pliers.

"Forbes," I said. "She walked in right in front of you. How could any of us? . . ."

"He here with you?" Forbes said, nodding at Shelly, who plunged his hands in his pockets to protect his fingers.

"Yes," I said.

"No," Pook stepped in helpfully. "He came late, just before the lady."

Shelly's mouth was open. He had lost his cigar. His brow was wet and he was shaking his head no and looking to me for salvation.

"Got it," Lou Canton called from the door.

Forbes turned his eyes to me. They were very gray, very cold eyes.

"That's two bucks extra for repairs," Lou said, moving past us without noticing Luna's body in the middle of the floor. "Plus it cost me two bucks plus to take a Red-Top cab here from Glendale."

"You weren't supposed to come today, Lou," I reminded him.

Lou glanced at the trembling Shelly and said, "You teach her to dance and you can keep my pay."

Lou was back working on the piano when he finally took a good look in our direction and saw the bloody Luna on the floor. He calmly began to collect his music and put it back in his portfolio.

"I just realized," he said, facing us. "I wasn't supposed to come today."

"Nobody moves. Nobody leaves and nobody speaks," Forbes said.

We all stood quietly while Forbes knelt, touched Luna's hair, and muttered so low that I was the only one who heard him, "You were a bitch and a half, lady, but you made me feel alive."

He stood up, adjusted the line of his trousers, and looked at each one of us to be sure he remembered.

"I start with the little fat one," he said, looking at Shelly, "and then the rest of you."

Lou strode over, his portfolio tucked under his thin arm, his toolbox in the other hand.

"What do I hear, threats?" he said. "You threatening me?"

"No, just shut up and go home, old man," Forbes said wearily before he turned and pointed to me. "You know what Luna was to me?"

"Yes," I said.

"No," said Forbes. "You do not. She was nothing to me. I barely knew the lady. And that's what I plan to tell the cops. And that's what you tell the cops."

"Why?" said Lou. "You already said you're gonna kill them all. You gonna kill 'em twice if they tell the cops you were bouncing the babe?"

"I told you to go home, old man."

"I'm going home," Lou said. "Peters, drop by with cash and hand it to me if you still have fingers."

And Lou was gone.

"Eight floors over our heads my wife is sleeping after a long night of making my life miserable," Forbes said. "She is why I am telling you that I barely knew Luna. Play this on my side and maybe I'll let the three of you live. But the fat one goes."

"Sounds like a good deal to me," said Pook.

"Me too," said Jerry.

"Look at him, Forbes," I said, pointing to Shelly. "He's a goddamn dentist."

"She pointed to him?" he asked.

"Yes," said Jerry helpfully.

"Enough for me," said Forbes. "He goes and your Fred Astaire goes with him. If Luna hadn't got this thing in her head about Astaire . . ."

He looked down at Luna once more, shook his head, and left the ballroom with Kudlap Singh two steps behind him.

"Don't touch anything and don't leave," I told my quivering crew. "I'm calling the cops."

"Forbes said . . ." Jerry started as I walked toward the double doors.

"I'm calling the cops," I repeated. "Shelly, go sit down and have a glass of water."

"Fingers," Shelly mumbled, looking at his hands. "Fingers. I'm a dentist. I need my fingers."

"He said he was going to kill you," Pook said helpfully. "Not cut off your fingers."

"He could do both," Shelly answered defiantly.

I went to make my call. There was a pay phone in the carpeted hallway. No sign of Forbes or the Beast of Bombay. I called the Wilshire District station and got a woman's voice I didn't recognize. I asked for Lieutenant Pevsner or Lieutenant Seidman. She asked me why. I said, "homicide," and she put me through to my brother.

"Pevsner," he answered as if someone had just jolted him from a nap and he didn't like being jolted.

"Toby," I said.

"I'm in the middle of something," Phil said. "Call back."

"Murder," I said.

A long nothing on the other end and then a resigned sigh and, "Who's dead?"

"Woman named Luna Martin. Ballroom of the Monticello Hotel. A few minutes ago."

"Stay there," he said and hung up.

I went back to the ballroom. Pook was leaning against a wall, arms folded. He glared at me when I came in. Jerry and Shelly were sitting on the edge of the bandstand. Jerry wouldn't meet my eyes. Shelly would. He pointed at me and said, "You are going to get me killed. I volunteered to help you and you are going to get me killed."

"No one is going to kill you, Shel," I said.

"And who's going to stop him?" Shelly said, trying to keep his glasses on his nose. "These actors? Gunther, who's two feet tall?"

"Gunther's out of town," I said. "And he's more than three feet tall."

"Ah, so you're going to keep me alive with a full supply of fingers? Comforting," he said, turning to Jerry, who ignored him. "I can sleep nights now. Toby Peters is on the case."

The four of us waited, trying not to look at the beautiful corpse, until Phil, Steve Seidman, and two uniformed officers showed up twenty minutes later.

Phil, a block of a man with short steely-gray hair, came in first. His tie was loose and his jacket was open, but reasonably pressed. My sister-in-law, Ruth, saw to that. There was a look of annoyance on Phil's face that looked uncannily like the look on his face in the photograph in my office. Steve Seidman, a thinning-haired scrawny man, was four or five steps behind Phil, as he had been since they had become partners two decades earlier. Phil waved the uniformed cops back to the double door and moved to the body.

"Luna Martin," he said, looking down at her.

"Right," I said, nodding to Seidman.

"Girlfriend of Fingers Intaglia," Phil went on.

"A fact which everyone seems to know with the possible exception of Mrs. Intaglia," I said.

"What happened?" Phil said.

"We got here about . . ." I began, but Phil cut me off with, "Not you and not the crying dentist. You." He pointed to Pook.

"Jerry and I have nothing to do with this," Pook said. "Peters hired us to come here this morning and look tough. We're actors. A few minutes after we got here this woman staggers in, points to him, and falls dead right there."

"I don't know her," Shelly protested, crossing his heart.

"Well," said Phil to Seidman, "if the dentist crosses his heart, he must be telling the truth. Go home, Minck. You're clear."

Shelly looked at me hopefully.

"He's being sarcastic, Shel," I said.

Shelly groaned.

"Just the four of you here?" said Phil.

"Five," I said, pointing to Luna.

"Six," Pook amended. "The old piano player."

"I'm corrected," Phil said, moving to the table and sitting.

"What about Intaglia?" Shelly said, looking at me, Pook, and Jerry.

"What about him?" Phil said, pouring himself a glass of no-longer-iced water.

"He was here with a Jap giant," Shelly said. "He threatened to kill me, to kill us all, to kill Fred Astaire."

"Dentists have access to all kinds of drugs," Seidman said wearily.

"I'm not . . . I don't take drugs," Shelly cried. "Tell them, Toby."

"He doesn't take drugs," I said.

"Was Intaglia here?" Phil asked.

"Arthur Forbes and a man named Kudlap Singh came in right after Luna," I explained.

"And they left?" Phil asked.

"They left," I agreed.

"Steve," Phil said.

"Check," said Steve.

It didn't take more when you've worked with someone almost every day for two decades. Seidman herded Shelly, Pook, and Jerry over to the bandstand. Then he took them individually up to the piano, where he interviewed them in a whisper the others couldn't hear.

"The piano player?" asked Phil.

"He took a cab back to Glendale," I said. "He's over eighty."

"What are you doing here, Toby?" my brother asked, rubbing his forehead.

"I was supposed to give Miss Martin a dancing lesson," I said.

Phil looked at his palms and then rubbed them together. "There's almost nothing I can say to that," he said, "but it's my job, so I'm going to try. You're a private investigator, not a dance teacher. Besides that, you can't dance."

"I faked it," I said. "Fred Astaire gave me some tips."

"Fred Astaire."

"Shelly was right. Fred Astaire hired me to get Luna Martin to stop demanding that he teach her to dance. And when Luna Martin has a boyfriend like Fingers Intaglia . . ."

"Let's call him Arthur Forbes," Phil suggested. "And sit down. I don't like looking up at you."

"Hurts to sit," I said. "Forbes's bodyguard, the Beast of Bombay, hit me in the ass."

"Should I ask why?"

"A warning to Fred Astaire."

"It's all clear now except for one thing," he said. "Who killed Luna Martin?"

"I don't know who or why or how."

"Astaire didn't maybe hire someone who got carried away?" Phil asked and then, with amazing restraint for my brother, added, "Will you for chrissake sit down? I don't care who hit you."

I eased myself onto the chair across from him, biting my lower lip and wishing I had brought the pillow in from the Crosley.

"Phil, would I kill someone? Kill a woman who was giving my client a hard time?"

"I didn't mean you," he said, looking toward the bandstand.

"They didn't even know why they were here. Do I need to call Marty?"

Martin Leib was my lawyer. "My" is a little too strong, since I didn't give him much business and what little I gave him required payment in advance. Martin Leib was a mercenary. Martin Leib looked at me and talked to me as if I were an annoying insect. Martin Leib was a hell of a good lawyer.

"No," said Phil, starting to get up, as a man with a small leather bag from the medical examiner's office and a trio of uniformed policemen came in. One cop was carrying a rolled-up stretcher over his shoulder. Another had a camera. Phil looked over at Seidman, who nodded. Phil got up and so did I.

"What now?" I asked.

"Now, you go home or wherever you go," said Phil wearily. "And I talk to hotel staff, Fred Astaire, and Mr. Arthur Forbes."

"Mr. Arthur Forbes, not Fingers Intaglia?"

"In this town," said Phil. "Arthur Forbes is spoken to politely."

"By you?"

"I don't know. I've never met the man."

This was not my brother. My brother Phil had a lifelong vendetta against all felons, all crime. In spite of his lousy temper and honesty, he had made it to the rank of captain and actually headed the Wilshire District for a couple of years. He was forced to step down as head of the Wilshire when he couldn't be polite to important people in the community and he couldn't keep his fists off of suspects.

"Phil," I said as he shooed me out of the ballroom. "This is Fingers Intaglia."

"I like catching criminals," he said. "I want to keep catching them. It helps me stay calm with my family. I have been informed by the chief of police that if I have one more complaint I'll be suspended without pay. So I'm going to do my best to be nice to Arthur Forbes."

We were in the hallway now, right in front of the phone I'd called him from.

"Okay," I said.

"Hell, it's not okay," Phil said, plunging his hands into his pockets to keep them still. "But I'm going to do it, Toby."

"This is crazy," called Shelly, as Seidman hurried him down the corridor.

Pook and Jerry went quietly. Both of them gave me a look which made it clear I shouldn't come to them for help again. But I knew better. Actors, even successful ones, which Pook and Jerry were not, would pretend they were the toilet cleaners at Grauman's Chinese Theater if it was the best role they could get.

"Can I ask?" I said, holding up my hands. "Don't get mad. How are Ruth and the kids?"

In the past, this simple family question had driven Phil to violence. He never clearly explained why, other than that I had given little or no thought to them when they needed me. I had made an effort to be a better brother-in-law and uncle since Ruth got sick. She had been in and out of the cancer ward for more than a year now. She seemed to be getting better, but it was slow and she never carried the weight for a good fight.

"They're fine," he said.

"Good. Phil, how quiet are you going to keep this?"

"Arthur Forbes is an important citizen," he said, looking back toward the ballroom. "I think the chief will be happy to keep this investigation confidential. At least for a while."

It wasn't Forbes I was worried about and Phil knew it. It was Fred Astaire. The guy from the medical examiner's office came out, following two guys lugging a stretcher. A gray blanket covered the body of Luna Martin. A corner of her silk dress fluttered as they carried her past Phil and me. The fabric brushed against my hand. And she was gone.

The medical examiner was a twig named O'Neil whose hair was never combed and whose glasses were never clean. He paused next to us, nodded at me, and said, "In front of him?"

Phil shrugged, hands out of his pockets now, searching for something to do with them.

"Suit yourself," O'Neil said. "Lady's throat was cut, nice thin, even stroke. She was also strangled, but there are no bruises. Not sure which killed her. I'll know more about the weapon and the cause of death sometime tonight or tomorrow morning. I've got bodies piling up. Riot, gangs, something in Little Mexico. I'll get to the little lady as fast as I can."

"Thanks," said Phil.

O'Neil was shaking his head and looking down the corridor in the direction Luna's body had been carried. "Seidman says it looks like she walked all the way into the middle of the ballroom after she had been attacked," he said.

"Right," I said.

"She couldn't have come far," said O'Neil. "A miracle that she could walk at all. That was a dead woman walking. I'd say she was murdered right out here, in front of the door to the ballroom probably. That was some determined woman."

"Amen," I said.

O'Neil strode down the corridor. When the M.E. was gone, Phil walked back to the door of the ballroom and looked down at the carpet. There were a couple of dark spots that might have been blood. There was no knife, nothing that looked like a murder weapon. On the chance that the killer had hidden the weapon, Phil looked behind the mirrors and paintings down the hall and went into the men's room.

"You want me to help?" I asked, standing behind him.

"You're a witness," he said. "Don't touch. Don't help."

Phil didn't need my assistance. When he was done, he went to the sinks against the wall, turned on the cold water full blast, and when the basin was half full he plunged his face into it and held it there for about five seconds. When he came up for air, he shook his head like a wet dog and dried his face with one of the towels piled in the corner. I'd watched this before. He had never explained the rite. I had tried it myself but it didn't seem to work the same magic for me. Phil looked refreshed.

"Time to see Mr. Forbes and his friends," he said.

"Let's go," I said.

"You go home. I see Mr. Forbes. We're getting along just fine so far. Let's not test it right now."

"Phil, I . . ."

"Go now, Tobias."

I went, but not out of the hotel. I hid behind some plants in the lobby. Phil went to the desk, where Seidman joined him. They talked to a clerk and headed for the elevator. When the elevator doors had firmly closed, I ran for the phone in the corridor near the ballroom and called the number Fred Astaire had given me. A man answered and I identified myself and asked for Astaire, telling him I thought it was important. Astaire came on about ten seconds later.

"Peters?"

"Luna Martin's dead."

He listened quietly while I told him what had happened, let him know that the police would be talking to him, and informed him that it probably wouldn't make the papers.

"I should have given her the damned lessons," Astaire said.

"I'd say the odds are very good that Luna Martin's death had nothing to do with you, me, or her dancing lessons."

"But Arthur Forbes doesn't think so."

"No, he doesn't."

"Then I'll have a talk with Arthur Forbes," said Astaire. "I don't want you or your friends getting hurt because you work for me."

"I don't think it'll do any good and it might be dangerous. Why don't I try to see him? Talk to him."

"A very good idea," came a deep accented voice behind me.

I turned and found myself looking up into the face of Kudlap Singh.

Chapter Five

Let's Dance

The big Indian didn't say another word. He walked slightly in front of me, certain that I wouldn't run and I wouldn't try to make my own impression on his behind. The man had confidence, good posture, and a poor choice in bosses.

He led me down the corridor to a door that brought us into the hotel kitchen. Two male cooks in white and a bellboy sat in one corner at a white metal table, talking and smoking. They looked up, saw Kudlap Singh, and went back to their conversation.

The smell of fried eggs, bacon, grilled sausage, and bananas accompanied us past the reasonably clean wooden cutting and serving tables and the metal sinks. We went through another door and into a small service area where an elevator stood open, waiting for us. Singh stepped aside so I could get on and then he followed, facing forward, and pressed a button. We jerked upward.

"Read any good books lately?" I asked.

"*They Were Expendable*," he answered, without turning.

He was not only bigger than I was, he was funnier. I shut up and we went up. A jerk-stop on eight and the Indian stepped out and waited for me. I followed him down a carpeted hotel corridor to room 813. Singh knocked and waited for Forbes's "Come in."

We entered, Singh behind me. It was a normal hotel sitting room with a closed door to the left, which I assumed was the bedroom. The dark, flower-patterned sofa had its back to the sunny floor-to-ceiling draped window and there were two matching chairs facing the sofa. There was an old, highly polished wooden table and two chairs in a corner. On top of the polished table sat a cake-box sized chrome metal box with a cord running out of it. On one wall hung a painting of a guy in one of those white colonial wigs.

"Admiring the painting?" Forbes said from where he sat, knees crossed and arms spread over the back of the sofa.

With the sun at his back, Forbes was a black cutout, which was probably what he wanted.

"Yes," I said, standing about six feet in front of him. "Washington."

"Thomas Jefferson," he corrected. "Jefferson and Washington didn't look anything alike, for chrissake. Painting of Jefferson in every guest room. I'd change the name of the hotel to the Thomas Jefferson if there wasn't already a Jefferson in Los Angeles. So I renamed it for his home, Monticello. You know he planned every brick in Monticello?"

"No," I said, preferring the history lesson to what he might have planned after it.

"Do you know it took him thirty-five years to build Monticello?"

"No," I said again.

"Do you know he started the University of Virginia? Not only did he found it, he designed the buildings."

"I didn't know that," I said, looking at Kudlap Singh, who showed no sign of whether or not he knew the accomplishments of Thomas Jefferson.

"In my home I've got furniture from Monticello, books,"

Forbes went on. "I tell you, I was born too late. In my heart I know I should have been around for the Revolution."

"Maybe you could buy the Jefferson Hotel," I suggested.

"Too high profile," he said. "I like to do things without drawing attention to myself. You want a drink?"

"Pepsi," I said.

"Fridge over behind the table. Help yourself. Kudlap Singh doesn't serve. He gets paid for only one thing. To keep me alive and well and in a good safe mood."

I went to the fridge, crouched, got a Pepsi out from a rack of wine and pop bottles. I stood up, looking for an opener. Kudlap Singh took the bottle from my hand and flipped the cap off with a thumb that looked like calloused leather.

"Jefferson was nothing like Washington," Forbes continued as I sat in one of the chairs facing him and gulping at my Pepsi. "Never went to battle. Jefferson was a blue blood, class. Grew up without a father, like me. When he was twenty-six, he was elected to the Colonial legislature of Virginia. When I was twenty-six, I was invited to join a well-known Detroit organization. Jefferson came up with the best ideas for the Declaration of Independence. I came up with a nonwritten agreement with all the organizations in Michigan, Minnesota, and Wisconsin. Jefferson was governor of Virginia twice, and I was head of the organization for two years."

"Similarities are uncanny," I said.

Forbes nodded and Kudlap Singh slapped me in the head. The right side of my head rang cold and metallic. I looked at Forbes, who hadn't moved.

"You make wise with me and you make pain for yourself. Got me?"

"Got you," I said.

"Pepsi cold enough? Need a glass, some ice, anything?"

"I'm fine," I said, trying to force my eyes back into coordinated operation.

"One time," he went on, "Jefferson missed by five minutes being captured by Tarleton's raiders. Same thing happened to me."

"Tarleton's raiders missed you by five minutes, too?" I asked, gripping the cool glass of the half-full Pepsi bottle, ready to take a swing at Kudlap Singh if he took another slap at me. I was sure the bottle would boink off of his head with no effect, but I was ready to try it. I watched Forbes for a nod. It didn't come.

"You know what your problem is, Peters? You've got guts and no brains," he said. "I'm talking history and I'm coming to a point, if you'll just shut up and listen and sit down."

"I'm listening," I said, sensing Kudlap Singh right over my shoulder.

I eased myself into one of the chairs in front of Forbes. The pain on my rear wasn't nearly as bad as it had been. I'd describe it now as the searing horror of a branding iron.

"I built my own place back in Royal Oak, exact duplicate of Monticello. I like to garden, read. What color are my eyes?" Forbes asked.

"Your eyes?"

"That's what I said."

"I can't see them," I said, squinting into the sun.

"Hazel," he said. "Like Jefferson. And when I was a kid I had sandy red hair like him. Can you believe that?"

"I'll take your word," I said.

"Nobody much knows this, but Jefferson had some lady friends," Forbes went on a little more softly. "Mostly Negro women. Slaves. Even had kids by them. A lot of the black Jeffersons you see cleaning your house, dancing in the movies, are descendants of the third president of the United States."

"I thought that was because their families and slave owners had admired Jefferson," I said.

"Some of that, too," Forbes said, waving off this line of thinking with an impatient hand. "This was Luna's room. Look around."

I looked around and my eyes met those of Kudlap Singh, who wasn't looking around. He was looking straight at me.

"Doesn't look lived in, does it?" he said. "Looks a little more like it in the bedroom, but . . ."

A long moment of silence while Forbes's head turned to look at the portrait of Jefferson before he went on.

"My wife is two stories up in the presidential suite. That's where we stay when we're in town. Right now I figure your brother the cop is talking to her, and she's finding out for sure that Luna Martin died in this hotel. Some point soon I'm gonna have to talk to the cops and talk to Carlotta. I'd rather face Bataglia or one of the boys from Chicago than talk to Carlotta about this. Carlotta's a pack rat. She never lets go of anything—a grudge, an old dress."

I nodded in understanding and sipped my Pepsi.

"What I said in the ballroom," he went on. "I was hot. I'm not killing anybody, you, the fat guy with the glasses, the two actors. I've got one person to kill. That's whoever murdered Luna. Cops are going to look for the killer. I'm gonna look for the killer. You are gonna look for the killer. One of us is gonna find the killer fast. You find him and you get five thousand cash."

"I've got a client," I said.

"Now you've got two clients," Forbes said, a note of irritation creeping into his voice as he took an envelope from his jacket pocket and pushed it toward me.

"Can't," I said. "Fred Astaire's my client and his case is mixed up in this. I'd need his permission."

"I can fix it so you'll never learn to play the harpsichord," said Forbes.

"I can always do war drums with my fist," I said.

"I think you don't understand, Peters. I think Kudlap will have to explain it to you." Forbes nodded.

I turned, fingers around the now-empty Pepsi bottle as the Indian took a step toward me. I started to get out of the chair. Singh put the envelope in my shirt pocket as someone knocked at the door. Kudlap Singh stopped and looked at Forbes, who said, "Who is it?"

"Room service."

"I don't want room service," Forbes said irritably.

"Then I'm Admiral Nimitz," the voice beyond the door said.

I recognized the voice. I raised an eyebrow at Forbes. He looked at me and with a deep sigh said, "Let him in."

Kudlap Singh went to the door, opened it, and Fred Astaire strode in, glanced around, and plunged his hands in his pockets. He was wearing a tweedy sport jacket, a white shirt, and a blue handkerchief tied around his neck. Kudlap Singh closed the door and put his back to it.

"Mr. Forbes, I—" Astaire began.

"How'd you find me?" Forbes cut him off.

"When Mr. Peters hung up in the middle of our telephone conversation, I came right over here, inquired, and found a maid whose name will be forever a secret who gladly exchanged the number of the room you were in for the promise of an autographed photo of me and Ginger."

"You came to rescue Peters," Forbes said.

"To try," Astaire said, patting down his remaining hair and looking around the room, his eyes coming to rest on the portrait on the wall. "Jefferson was supposed to be a superb minuet dancer," said Astaire admiringly.

"I know," said Forbes. "Now we cut the shit. Luna's dead.

You were supposed to teach her to dance. Now she's dead. She had a big mouth. She was a pain in the ass, but she was a good kid and a great . . . cops are gonna be all over me and my people and my wife."

"I'll be happy to talk to your wife and the police," Astaire said sincerely. "Miss Martin's death may well have something to do with my refusal to teach her. I can't help thinking that she might be alive if I had come and faced her directly."

"It was hard to say no directly to Luna," Forbes said.

"You can't believe Peters or his associates had anything to do with this," Astaire said.

"I can believe what I want to believe," Forbes said, finally moving his arms. "And I know I want you to tell Peters to start looking for Luna's killer. The cops give me a choice—go big with this and look for the killer, knowing that the papers will get it; or go small, keep the publicity down, and maybe never find him. Or, if they do like they do in Detroit, they find someone, shoot him in an alley with two guns in his hands, and lay every murder in the last year on his bloody chest. You want headlines like, 'Astaire Involved in Investigation of Murdered Blonde He Was Teaching to Dance'?"

"It's too long for a headline, but you have a point," Astaire said.

"You want your wife, your kids, the studio to know you got involved in something like murder?" Forbes continued.

Astaire's hands were out of his pockets now, but Forbes was unimpressed.

"You don't know much about me, Fingers," Astaire said.

Forbes shook his head and said, "Five-nine, weigh a hundred and thirty-eight or thirty-nine pounds fully dressed. Brown eyes. When you're not working, you wear two-piece underwear. When you do a dance number, you wear a union suit. You're mild-mannered and hard to burn, but when you blow you've got a bad temper and you break furniture and anything handy. Might something handy include a big-mouthed blonde who wants you to teach her to dance and won't take no for an answer?"

"Look, Forbes," Astaire said angrily, not noticing that Kudlap Singh had stepped away from the door and toward us.

"Maybe we should—" I began, but Forbes went on, pushing: "Your shirts, underwear, pajamas, and dressing gowns are monogrammed and you have a hell of a time each morning deciding what tie to wear. You and your wife sleep in separate beds. You wear silk, usually blue, pajamas, and you wiggle your toes in your sleep. Your wife's name is Phyllis and your kids—"

"You son of a bitch," Astaire said, frail body shaking, hands in a fist.

Forbes seemed amused.

"You want a career, feet, a family," he said, pointing at Astaire, "see to it that he finds who killed Luna because I'm gonna tell you something personal about me. I loved Luna and I don't like it that someone killed her. I don't like it at all. I want the bastard caught and brought to me. I don't care who finds him. That's what I want."

"You two-bit Capone," Astaire said as I stepped between him and Forbes, who didn't even get up.

"Capone, between you and me, was a publicity-seeking blowhard who didn't control half of what we had in Detroit." Now Forbes rose, let out a sigh, and straightened the creases in his trousers. "Sit down, calm down, and think things over," he said, moving past me and Astaire and toward the door with the Indian. "You'll hear from me."

And then they were gone.

"He threatened me, my wife, and my children," Astaire said, his face a distinct shade of red. "That fart-faced—"

"He's on his way to owning half of Los Angeles," I said.

"And I know the people who own the other half," Astaire countered hotly, now pacing the room. "And I think I'll have a talk with some of them."

"I think we should consider carefully before we say anything more," I said, pointing to the metal box on the table in the corner.

Astaire kept pacing and glancing at the box.

"That's not a listening device," he said. "It's a wire recorder. It has a microphone inside the box so you can record on spools of wire."

"You know how it works?" I asked, moving to the machine.

"Yes," he said, striding impatiently to my side, unhooking a clasp on the side of the box and lifting the lid.

There was a microphone inside with a wire wound round it and a spindle with a spool the size of a salt box fitted over it. Gray metal, most of it with thin lines across it, covered the spool.

"Would you say Luna recorded something on this wire?" I asked, looking at the thing.

"Somebody recorded something," Astaire said. "I'd guess Luna was copying songs from the radio."

"Or . . ." I said.

"Can't hurt," he said, and turned the machine on.

The quality wasn't bad.

There were two songs at the start of the recording. Astaire asked me if I knew what steps they were. I didn't. He told me they were a fox-trot and a rumba. After the second song, I said, "Let's go."

"We're here," he said. "We've got nothing better to do but

find a killer and talk to the police. The least we could do is hear the lady out."

I shrugged and moved back to lean against the wall as an announcer said, "Hello, we've been waiting for you. It's time to play 'Truth or Consequences.' "

This was followed by the bleating of Beulah the Buzzer and Ralph Edwards saying, "Aren't we devils."

I reached over to turn it off but Astaire stopped me. We kept listening. A woman and her husband were asked if a hen *sits* or *sets* when she lays an egg. Before the couple could answer and collect their fifteen dollars, Beulah squawked her into submission and a "consequence." Edwards then sent the wife off and had the husband dressed as a woman. The husband was placed behind a cashier's window, pretending he was the woman who was going to pay off the wife when she came back on stage. When the wife was brought back, Ralph Edwards offered her sixty dollars if she could find her husband, who was in plain sight in the small studio. The woman lost one dollar for every second she didn't find him.

"I don't think—" Astaire said, and then a phone rang, a phone on the tape.

The audience was giggling and then the muffled sound of Luna answering the phone. It was hard to make out her words as the woman on the wire recording got more frantic, the audience laughed, and Edwards egged her on, but Luna's side of the conversation sounded like, "No . . . I'mmot . . . look Immot gnn peck to thad . . . no . . . no fke Tuesdip in any Hollywood stirfunt . . . [Laughter and Ralph Edwards too loud to hear this part, and then] . . . Yucatan tk yur post age sighs eggs ques fura bllrum and . . . don thread on me. Cumner me anfingersll tarut yurhert . . . [Phone is hung up]."

"Truth or Consequences" went on with the wife on the radio crying frantically, "Where are you?"

Luna, now closer to the microphone, said something fast and turned off the machine.

The silver spool continued to run with a hum. Astaire reached over and rewound it.

He listened to Luna's side of the phone conversation once more and turned off the machine.

"Did you understand what she said?" he asked.

"Not much."

"It's like doing a bad loop in a cheap studio. She said, 'Look, I am not going back to that. No fake two-step in any Hollywood storefront . . . You can take your postage-size excuse for a ballroom. . . . Do not threaten me. . . . Come near me, and Fingers will tear out your heart."

"Then she went to the machine," I continued. "And in answer to the contestant's question, 'Where are you?' answered 'Where you'll never have the nerve to find me, Willie.'"

"So . . ." Astaire began, his hand to his chin.

"Willie may have had the nerve to find Luna," I said. "Find her and kill her."

"We're not sure what he threatened her with or about," said Astaire.

"And it probably has nothing to do with her murder," I went on.

"But then again . . ." Astaire said.

"I go looking for a Willie connected to a storefront ballroom."

"*We* go looking, and my guess is we're talking about a storefront dance studio, not a real ballroom. Probably the one where she supposedly taught."

"I don't want to argue but . . ."

"Look, Peters," he said, a hand to his chest and the other pointing at me. "I've been a police follower all my life, city to city, since I was a kid. Crime is more than a hobby with me. It's a passion. I'm going to help. It's my case too, remember."

"I thought you had a show and a bond tour."

"I've got a few days. When is 'Truth or Consequences' on?"

"Sunday, eight-thirty," I said.

"So Willie called her Sunday at about ten minutes after eight. That means . . ."

The door flew open and a woman stormed in, dark and on fire.

"Where is he?" she asked.

She was little, no more than four-ten, pretty, long dark hair brushed straight and to her neck with evenly trimmed bangs across her forehead. She had on too much makeup and too few clothes. What she wore looked like a sarong held up by a pair of very full breasts.

"Who?" I asked as she started across toward the bedroom, suddenly stopped and turned around, red mouth open.

"Fred Astaire," she said.

"Caught," Astaire said with a winning smile.

The woman came back toward us.

"I've seen all your movies, even the one you did with Joan Crawford . . ."

"Dancing Lady," Astaire said. "Let me guess. You're Mrs. Forbes and you are looking for your husband."

"Yes," she said with a very forced smile. "The police have been asking me stupid, stupid questions for the last who-knows-how-long. And then, finally, they tell me that someone killed the little . . . . Who are you? What are you both doing in this room?"

"You know Mr. Astaire," I said. "I'm Toby Peters, private investigator. Your husband wants to hire me to find Miss Martin's killer."

She shook her head and went for the bedroom door, throwing it open with a bang.

"He's not here," she said after going in, checking, and coming out with a blue-silk robe. "But he was. This is his. I saw her three times. Cheap. Didn't know how to use eyeliner."

She looked at Astaire again, who stood there bouncing on his heels, arms folded, looking pleased with the world.

"What do you have to do with all this?" she asked Astaire.

"I was giving Miss Martin dance lessons."

"That bastard," Mrs. Fingers Forbes shouted, her red fingernails turning to curled, ready claws.

She bounced to the door, turned, and said, "I'm really not like this. It's just that . . ."

"We understand," said Astaire.

"If you could teach her to dance, you could teach me."

"Well, I . . ."

"I'll talk to Arthur about it," she said in a tone that made it clear that neither Arthur nor Astaire would have a choice in the matter.

"I really can't take . . ." Astaire began, but she was out and gone.

"I suggest we lock the door," I said. "We check the bedroom fast, take the recording, and get the hell out of here."

Five minutes later we were out the door and I had stolen a towel from the Monticello. The towel was loosely wrapped around the wire recording. Fred Astaire bounced along at my side. We met no one in the hall and no one in the nearly empty lobby.

When we stepped out onto the street, we finally met somebody: the two uniformed cops who had come with Phil and Steve Seidman. They stepped in front of us, blocking our escape.

"Mr. Astaire," said the younger of the two—much, much

younger, teeth still a bright, natural white. "I'm sorry, but I'll have to ask Mr. Peters to come with us."

"I don't see why you have to apologize to him," I said, nodding at Astaire. "We're not together. He was just walking out at the same time . . ."

"Now, wait a minute," Astaire said.

The second cop was much older, much more experienced, and much more stupid than the young one.

"Inside," he said, taking my arm. "We were told to get you. Mr. Laurel, here, can leave."

"This's Fred Astaire, Tim," the younger cop whispered.

"I don't care if he's King Kong. He can dance in the street for nickels and wait out here."

A crowd was gathering. Some of them clearly recognized Astaire.

"I'll call you later," I said.

Astaire nodded and went for a taxi at the curb.

Steve Seidman, gaunt and weary, stood at the end of the lobby near the corridor leading to the ballroom. His hands were behind his back as the two cops ushered me toward him.

"I'll make a deal with you, Toby," he said. "You give me the towel and whatever's in it that you took from Luna Martin's room, and I'll give you something in return."

I handed him the towel and the wire recording. His hands came out from behind his back and he handed me some sheet music.

"One of your extras posing as tough guys says you had an old piano player who may have left these here. They were on the piano."

I took them.

"Thanks," I said. "Lou's old, forgets things."

Seidman nodded, not caring.

"You can go," he said, taking the spool out of the open towel.

I eased past the two cops and left the Monticello. When I got outside I opened the envelope Forbes had pushed on me. It held five new hundred-dollar bills. I was in search of a storefront dance studio and a guy named Willie. I had often had less to work with, but this time I had a lot of incentive.

Chapter Six

Everybody Do the Varsity Drag

There were fourteen places calling themselves dance studios or ballrooms in the L.A. phone book. I went to a candy store with a stack of nickels and started phoning around, leaving the big ones for last. While I called I munched on a mound of marble halvah and watched the traffic go by on Sunset.

"Make Believe Ballroom," came a world-weary woman's voice on the first call.

"I'd like to talk to Willie."

"We have no Willie," she said.

"How about William or Bill?"

"No," she said with a sigh. "Are you interested in dance lessons?"

"No thanks," I said. "I just had one with Fred Astaire."

"Give him my best," she said and hung up.

My rear end still smarting and my stomach aching from too much halvah and a desperate need for a Pepsi, I kept dialing—Mr. Lyon's Studio of Dance, Terpsicorean Interludes, the Royal Ballroom, Corine's House of Dance, the Talented Two-Step, Harold Augustine's Dance Studio, the Viennese Ballroom.

After seven tries, I'd found one Bill and a Willie. Bill turned out to be a Negro about seventy who cleaned up at the studio and other shops on the block. The conversation with Willie was even less promising. Willie was a woman. I struck Willie-gold on the eighth call.

"On Your Toes Dance Studio and College," the man answered sleepily.

He sounded very much like the man on Luna's wire recording.

"I'd like to speak to Willie," I said.

"Concerning?"

"Dance lessons."

"Who are you?"

"My name is Toby Peters," I said.

"This is William Talbott," he said.

"I want to dance."

"We want to teach you," said Willie. "Who gave you my name?"

"Your name?"

"You asked for 'Willie.'"

"A friend who's familiar with your studio."

"Took lessons with us?"

"Learned a great deal from you."

"And recommended us?"

"You specifically," I said lightly.

"This person's name might not be Stella?"

"It might well be."

"That explains it," he said. "I'm at your service, Mr . . ."

"Peters, Toby Peters. When can we start?"

"Anytime tomorrow," he said. "From nine in the morning till nine at night."

"How about today?"

"Today," he said. "Let me look."

He shuffled some papers and I waited. I had a feeling his answer would be—

"You're in luck. We have a cancellation this afternoon at two."

"Can we make it one?" I asked.

"Ah . . . that will be difficult, but I can make a few shifts and changes to accommodate a new student."

"Thank you."

"You know how to get here?"

The address was on Western, not far from Melrose.

"I'll be there at one."

We hung up. It was eleven-thirty in the morning. If I hurried, I could get to the On Your Toes Dance Studio and College and catch Willie when he wasn't on his toes.

I called my office. Violet answered, "Sheldon Minck, Creative Dentistry without Pain."

"And Toby Peters, Private Investigator," I said.

"Dr. Minck said I shouldn't give your name," Violet said.

"Put Dr. Minck on the phone."

"He doesn't want to talk to you, Mr. Peters," she whispered. "I wish you'd come here quick. He just sits in his dental chair looking at his fingers."

"I'll get there as soon as I can, Violet. Anything else?"

"You got a call from . . . a Miss Anita Maloney. She left a number. You want it?"

Maybe Anita wanted to go to another prom or she remembered I had borrowed two bucks from her on prom night. Violet gave me her number. I wrote it in my notebook even though I had it scrawled on a napkin somewhere in my pocket.

"And a Mr. Forbes called saying you should give him a call as soon as you checked in."

I heard a distinct background groan from Shelly Minck. I took Forbes's number.

"That it?" I asked.

"You owe me two dollars," she said.

"The fight," I remembered.

"Ortiz in a TKO over Salica in the eleventh. Double or nothing on the Bivins-Mauriello fight tomorrow?"

"Odds today?"

"Bivins is still five-to-six."

"You get Bivins. I get Mauriello. My ten to your two. You lose and we're even."

"Okay," she said brightly. "If Dr.—"

She was cut off by the phone being wrenched from her hand. The frantic voice of Sheldon Minck came crackling.

"My fingers are my life," he said, nearly weeping. "I'm like a . . . like a harpist, or an exterminator."

"What is so special about an exterminator's fingers?"

"You try using a Flit can with paws," Shelly said.

"No one is going to cut off your fingers," I said. "I talked to Forbes. All that was for show. He tried to hire me to find out who killed Luna."

"I didn't do it," Shelly cried.

"Until you said that I didn't suspect you."

"Said what?" Shelly screamed.

"I'm kidding, Shel," I said. "Your fingers are safe and I don't suspect you."

"You're lying to make me feel better."

"I'm not lying, Shel, but your fingers might be in trouble if you don't tell Violet to say my name when she answers the phone. We have an agreement."

"I'll tell her," he said reluctantly. "You sure I'm—"

"I'm sure, Shel."

"Then I can have Violet go down to Manny's and pick up some tacos."

"What has one thing got to . . . right, Shel. You can have Violet pick up some tacos. Good-bye."

I hung up and retrieved my Crosley from Cotton Wright, the parking attendant at the Monticello, and gave him a buck tip, which I marked in my expense book along with the cost of parking.

"You a veteran?" Cotton asked as I eased gently onto the pillow I had taken from my room at Mrs. Plaut's boarding-house.

"No, Cotton. You asked me that a few days ago."

"What did you answer?"

"No. I wasn't a veteran then and I'm still not."

"You know I've got a piece of metal in my head from the war?"

"I know, Cotton," I said, turning on the ignition.

"Sometimes it hurts. Sometimes it hums. Sometimes I don't even notice."

"What are the best times?" I asked.

"When it hums," he said.

I pulled out of the lot with a wave at Cotton and headed down Sunset, bound for Western. I turned on the radio and through the static learned that the Japanese had captured Hinajong in Northern Hunan in their drive southward over the Yangtze. On the other hand, the Chinese were making gains in Burma. I also learned that more meat rationing was coming April 1. Mrs. Plaut would be on me for that. I wondered whether Anita Maloney could come up with ground beef as easily as she came up with potatoes.

There was a small parking space only a car the size of a Crosley could love right near the corner of Western and Melrose. I backed into it, trying not to turn my body too painfully to look over my shoulder. When I was parked, I opened the door and eased out, my rear end a massive, low-level electric shock. But, all in all, it felt better than it had the day before.

The On Your Toes Dance Studio and College was not a storefront. It was in a small office building. I found it listed in the directory in a dark, white-tiled lobby the size of a small rest room. The white tile was seriously cracked, and the black-on-white list of offices and renters was badly in need of some letters. Next to the building directory was a yellowing poster that read, "Save Cooking Fats and Grease."

I found the studio between Nona's Hair and Fingernails and Quick Letter Copy Service. On Your Toes was on the ground floor. I groped my way past the narrow staircase and along an even narrower short corridor, at the end of which was a pebble-glass door with "On Your To s Danc Studio" printed in gold letters. A simple line drawing of a dancing couple had been drawn on the glass. The man wore a tuxedo. The woman wore a billowy white dress. They were both smiling. I knocked at the door. No answer. I waited. Knocked again. Still no answer. I tried the door. It was open. I walked into a room almost as dark as the hallway. The lights were out and the venetian blinds on the windows across the floor were closed. The only light that came into the room was through the spaces left by broken, bent, and missing slats on the blinds.

I was in a wooden-floored room about the size of a handball court. The wall of mirrors to my right made it look a little bigger, but the cracks in the mirrors worked against any possible suggestion of class. On my left was a glassed-in dark cubicle that must have been the office. I walked over to it and opened the door.

There was a crash from the end of the cubicle from somewhere just beyond the outline of a desk. I froze.

"Don't move," came a man's voice.

I could see enough of the man who rose behind the desk to see that he carried what looked like a gun in his right hand.

"I'm not moving," I said.

"Put your hands behind your head," he said.

I put my hands behind my head and a desk lamp snapped on, bouncing odd shadows.

The big man with the gun was about forty with full, ruffled blond hair and a frightened look on his face. He wore dark wrinkled trousers and a mess of a long-sleeved white shirt unbuttoned to show his undershirt.

"Who sent you?" he asked.

"Stella," I said.

"She's a whore," he said, voice cracking. "I don't owe her a goddamn nickel. Chavez sent you, or Albertini."

I kept my hands behind my head and watched him fumble through the mess on his desk until he found a pack of cigarettes. He managed to light one with trembling fingers and keep the gun aimed in the general direction of my chest.

"I told them I'd pay them a little at a time," Willie went on. "I've got a rich new student and I've been in touch with a friend with a lot of money."

"Luna Martin?" I guessed.

That almost stunned the cigarette from his lips.

"How did you . . . she owes me," he said, trying to compose himself and glancing from time to time at the door to my right.

"My name is Toby Peters," I said.

"Peters? You're a . . ." he said, looking at the alarm clock on his desk. "You're an hour early."

"Eager to dance," I said. "Can I take my hands down?"

"How did you know about Luna?" he asked suspiciously.

"She's a friend. She's the one who sent me here."

"Luna sent you here for dance lessons?"

"In a way," I said. "Hands down?"

"At your sides," he said. "But don't move. No offense, Peters, but I've got some people I owe a few dollars, and they won't handle this in a civilized manner. You understand?"

"Fully," I said. "Think you could put the gun down now?"

He looked at the gun in his hand and took the cigarette from his mouth. He placed the gun on the table in front of him.

"Bad start," he said with a smile as he brushed back his hair.

"I wouldn't say we hit it off on first sight," I agreed.

"Well," he went on, buttoning his shirt. "I was just taking a little nap to get the creative juices evenly divided throughout my body. All body liquids flow to your toes when you're standing unless your heart and the other organs keep them flowing through the body. That puts a strain on your heart."

"And the other organs," I added.

"That's right," he said, tucking in his shirt.

Someone or something groaned from behind the desk. Willie Talbott ignored the sound and said, "A dancer needs an even distribution of body liquids and an even disposition."

"And a gun," I said, taking a step to my left where I could see around the side of the desk.

A pair of bare feet, definitely female, were clearly visible.

"Miss Perez is recirculating her body fluids," Talbott said. "Clothes constrict the flow."

"Makes sense to me," I said. "She seems to be asleep."

"She's concentrating deeply," Talbott explained, putting the cigarette back in his mouth and coming from behind the desk. I eased farther to the left in the hope of seeing more of the meditating Miss Perez.

Talbott took my arm and guided me toward the door, removing the cigarette from his mouth again to tell me that I was in luck, On Your Toes was offering an introductory special, three lessons for five dollars. Each lesson was half an hour. Payment was required in advance. Results were guaranteed.

We were back on the wooden floor and out of the office now.

"In three lessons you'll have me dancing?" I asked.

"Guaranteed," he said, trying not to glance at the entrance door through which collection goons might suddenly charge, and at his office through whose window we might see the unclad Miss Perez rise.

Up close and with better light I revised my estimate of Willie Talbott. He was closer to my age and in need of a shave. His hair was definitely dyed. The gray stubble on his unshaven face was a giveaway.

"I can't hear the beat," I said.

"I could teach a deaf elephant," he said with a smile, showing impossibly white teeth.

"Fred Astaire gave up on me," I said.

"He doesn't have my patience," Talbott said with an amused smile.

"Okay," I said. "Then I have only one question."

"Payment in advance," he said. "Five dollars for three lessons. Otherwise, the special offer doesn't apply."

"No," I said. "You called Luna Martin a few days ago. What did you want from her?"

Talbott couldn't help looking at his desk through the window. Somewhere on that desk was his gun.

"Look," he said, taking a step back from me. "Tell Luna to just forget it. It was just a . . . a . . ."

"Gag," I said.

"Something like that," he agreed, looking for somewhere to put his cigarette.

He took a few steps toward his office door. I stopped him with, "Where were you this morning from ten to eleven?"

"This . . . right here. In my office. Meditating."

"On the floor?" I asked.

"Yes."

"With Miss Perez?"

"Yes."

"Let's talk to Miss Perez," I said.

"Look . . ." he began.

I smiled. I do not have a pleasant smile. He shuddered.

"What's this about?" Talbott tried.

"It's about someone cutting Luna Martin's throat this morning," I said.

Talbott backed away.

"No," he said.

"Yes," I said. "She used to work here."

"No," he said.

"She didn't work here?"

"Yeah, she worked here. I mean . . ." His hands were brushing back his hair furiously. "No, she can't be dead."

"What were you trying to blackmail her with?" I asked, advancing on Talbott, who took another step back.

"Blackmail her? Luna? I wasn't . . . I didn't," he said, looking around the empty little studio for sympathy or help.

"Luna recorded her conversation with you, Willie," I said. "The police have the wire. They're going to find you the way I found you. And they are going to ask you the same questions. Only, they won't be as sweet as I am."

"Shit, damn, crap," Talbott said, throwing what was left of his cigarette at the cracked mirror.

"And snap, crackle, pop," I added.

"It can't get any worse," he said helplessly.

But he was wrong.

The door behind me crashed open, rattling the glass. Talbott's eyes widened with terror as he stared over my shoulder at whoever had come in. I turned. The dancing couple on the door were quivering. Two men stood in the doorway. Both were big. Neither was well dressed, neither wore a hat, but who am I to talk. The shorter one was a bulldog. The bigger one a Saint Bernard.

"You ain't home," said the bulldog.

It was an observation that couldn't be challenged.

"I spent the night here," Talbott said, his voice cracking.

The Saint Bernard closed the door.

"Who's this?" the bulldog asked.

"A client," I said.

"Blow," the bulldog said to me.

"Peters, no," Talbott pleaded.

"Blow, client. Willie and us have business to talk about," said the bulldog.

"I'll tell you about Luna," Talbott almost wept, clutching my sleeve.

"How much does he owe you?" I asked.

The bulldog looked at me for the first time.

"He owes Mr. Chavez, Mr. Constantine Chavez, three thousand dollars," the bulldog said. "You got three thousand dollars, client?"

I was supposed to be impressed by the mention of Constantine Chavez. Normally, I would have been. Chavez was a middle-level mobster with a reputation for having no patience.

"No," I said, facing them, Talbott behind me. "But I work for a man who has, Arthur Forbes."

"Fingers?" the bulldog said suspiciously, turning to the Saint Bernard, who showed no emotion. The bulldog turned back to me and cocked his head. "What's Fingers got to do with this jamocko?" asked the bulldog.

"Mr. Forbes wants some information from him," I said. "Mr. Forbes may well be willing to pay three thousand dollars for the information."

Bulldog thought about this for a while. He examined our faces, turned once more to the Saint Bernard, who said, in a surprisingly high voice, "Chavez said we get the money or we break him up."

The bulldog sighed and nodded. "Asked you once, ask you again. You got the cash, client?"

"No," I said.

"Then we break him up. Tell Mr. Forbes we hope there's no hard feelings. We'll leave him so's he can still talk."

Talbott let out a pained gasp behind me.

"Hold it," I said, holding up my hands.

"We got a job," said bulldog. "Don't make it no harder than it is."

What happened next was fast and confusing, but I think I've got it straight. Bulldog was about two inches in front of me now. The Saint Bernard was at his side, looking at Talbott. I heard glass shatter and turned to Talbott's cubicle. The cubicle's window crashed to the floor, sending shards of glass in a burst in our direction. I covered my face with my arm and got a glimpse of a naked girl, undoubtedly Miss Perez, who had given up her meditation, had a gun in her hand, and was now firing at me, the bulldog and the Saint Bernard. I went to the floor. So did the bulldog and the Saint Bernard. Behind me I could hear Talbott letting out a series of strangled whimpers.

The cracked mirror on the far wall exploded with the second shot from Miss Perez. I covered my head, tasting glass shards on my lips as I tried to push through the wooden floor. There were four more shots, more breaking glass, and then the place went quiet, except for heavy breathing and Talbott's groaning.

We all got up slowly, gingerly brushing glass from our clothes and skin. Bulldog's forehead was bleeding. The Saint Bernard looked as if the palm of his right hand had been shredded. I seemed to be all right. We all looked at Miss Perez, who still held the pistol in her hands, aiming it in our direction. She was dark with long straight black hair. She was very pretty and she was very, very young and she was very naked. She should have been very scared as well, but she didn't look it. She just looked dazed and stood there blinking. I wondered what she and Talbott had been doing besides evening out their body liquids.

"This don't change nothing," bulldog said.

"Someone must be calling the cops right now," I tried.

"We work fast," said bulldog.

"We are professionals," added Saint Bernard.

"Oh, God," Talbott groaned behind me. "Peters."

"Look," I said.

Bulldog pushed me toward Saint Bernard, who punched me in the shoulder and sent me awfully damned close to stumbling into the jagged glass left in Talbott's cubicle window. Bulldog had Talbott by the neck now. Saint Bernard was watching me. I knew I was going to try something ridiculous and I was pretty sure I didn't have a chance in the world. I looked over at Miss Perez. Eighteen, tops, I figured, and started back toward the fugitives from the kennel.

"Pardon me," came a voice from the doorway.

Everyone in the room froze, then turned to the newcomer who stood in the doorway, hands on his hips.

"I have to tell you I've danced in worse," said Fred Astaire.

I looked at bulldog and Saint Bernard. A faint look of possible recognition touched the bigger man's face. The bulldog showed nothing.

"Get out, now," bulldog said. "Now."

"Can't do that," Astaire said with a smile, tiptoeing over broken glass.

"Throw him out," the bulldog said, and the Saint Bernard lumbered toward Astaire.

It was no contest. Astaire jumped to his right as the big man reached for him. Astaire threw a short, sudden kick to the rear of the big man's left knee, and the Saint Bernard went down with a grunt. Bulldog left Talbott and moved toward Astaire, who circled to his right, saying, "If we can just be reasonable."

Bulldog was in no mood to be reasonable and he was quicker on his feet than Saint Bernard. He anticipated Astaire moving to his left or right and had his arms held wide open. Astaire stepped into the open arms, planted his left foot flat on the floor, and leveled a stomach-high kick at the bulldog, who staggered back, slipped on glass, and fell heavily.

I moved to the Saint Bernard, who was doing his best to get to his feet and finding it hard to do without the support of his left leg. Bulldog was rolling on the floor, holding his stomach, and trying to catch his breath.

"I've never done anything like that in my life," Astaire said.

"I think we should get out of here," I said.

I grabbed the open-mouthed Willie Talbott and pushed him toward the door. Then I went into Talbott's office and moved toward Miss Perez, who backed away from me as I circled around the desk. I took the empty gun from her hand, put it on the desk, reached down, picked up a flowery dress from the floor, and handed it to her. She looked at the dress as if it were some alien and puzzling item from Mars.

"Put it on," I said. "Fast."

I glanced over my shoulder and saw Astaire and Talbott going through the studio door.

Miss Perez took the dress and got into it.

"You have shoes?" I asked. "You don't want to walk through this glass without shoes."

She blinked around at the floor, spotted a pair of slingback pumps, and slipped them on. I looked over at bulldog and Saint Bernard. They were recovering slowly, but they were recovering. I guided Miss Perez out of the cubicle and past the Saint Bernard, who turned to me and said, "I can't walk, I can't work."

"Should have thought of that before you became an insurance salesman," I said.

Astaire and Talbott were standing on the sidewalk. Talbott looked at Miss Perez, turned to me and said, "Let's get the hell out of here."

"How did you find me?" I asked Astaire.

"Wasn't looking for you," he said with a shrug. "I called Forbes and asked him if he knew the name of the dance studio where Luna taught before he met her. He told me and . . ."

"Here you are," I said. "Thanks."

"Let's not do it again," he said, looking at Miss Perez.

"Talbott's right," I said. "We should get out of here. I can only take one passenger in my Crosley."

Astaire led us around the corner to a big black Lincoln with darkened windows. I kept my hand on Talbott's shoulder to discourage him from taking off down the street. Astaire had no trouble leading Miss Perez to the front seat.

Fifteen minutes later we dropped Miss Perez at her aunt's apartment on Burnside. Astaire gave her two twenty-dollar bills and asked if she was going to be all right.

Miss Perez had managed to find her way halfway back to the planet and, as she got out of the car, twenties in hand, she looked at Fred Astaire and said, "You're him."

"Always have been," Astaire said.

"Is it okay I tell my Tia Alicia?" she asked.

"It would be my pleasure," Astaire said as she opened the door.

"I don't think I'm gonna spend this money ever," she said.

"I suggest you do spend it," said Astaire.

"Well," she said, stepping onto the curb and brushing

back a stray strand of hair. "Maybe one of them. Sorry I tried to kill you."

I waved a hand in my best nonchalant manner.

"Willie?" she said to Talbott, but his head was down and he was in no mood for words of love.

Astaire pulled away from the curb and looked at Talbott and me in the rearview mirror.

"Well, Mr. Peters, where do we go from here?"

Chapter Seven

The Last Waltz

"What were you threatening Luna Martin with?" I asked, biting into my hot dog.

"Pardon me?" Willie Talbott answered.

I finished my dog, a giant Poochie Dog with kraut and a Pile-O-Fries from the Tastee Pup, a stand on Washington shaped like a giant Collie. Sandwiches were served over the counter in the dog's belly. We—Fred Astaire and Willie Talbott—sat at one of the four wooden tables next to the dog. A couple of young women dressed for office work kept looking over at us, trying to decide if the man in sunglasses and Greek fisherman's cap was someone famous.

Astaire sat with his legs crossed, facing Talbott. Astaire's dog was naked, no ketchup, no nothing, just a red dog on a bun. I stood at his side next to the table, reaching down for my fries. My rear was only slightly improved. It felt better to stand.

"When I was a kid, I mean back in Seattle, they used to call me Twinkle-Toes, Twinkle-Toes Talbott," Talbott said, wolfing down onion rings and looking over his shoulder for the Saint Bernard and the bulldog. "I had this talent with my feet, could pick up, improvise, show people how to do it."

"Twinkle-Toes," Astaire said, putting down his hot dog, "what were you threatening Luna Martin with?"

"Luna wasn't much of a dancer," Talbott said, looking at my side of fries now that his pile was exhausted. "But she looked good and she wanted to learn. So, we made a deal. You know what I mean?"

"Like the deal you have with Miss Perez?" I asked.

"Something like that," he said. "You mind?" He pointed at my fries. I shrugged. He took a handful.

"And you taught her how to dance?" Astaire asked.

"Everything she knew," Talbott said. "And she showed no gratitude, no loyalty, no appreciation. You think I might have another dog? I left all my money back in the office."

Astaire fished his wallet out and handed Talbott a buck.

"Be right back," he said and hurried to the open stomach of the collie, who looked suspiciously like Lassie, though Vivian Starbuck who owned the place insisted when asked that it was just a coincidence. "All collies look alike," she said. "Mine just happens to look more like Lassie."

"Having Luna Martin teach people to dance is like asking Hitler to teach the principles of Buddhism," Astaire said, watching Talbott who stood patiently waiting for his food. "Maybe we should have let those two back there shoot him."

"You mean it?"

"No," said Astaire, looking at me over his sunglasses. "But the Twinkle-Toes Talbotts of the world are unleashing a plague of lead-footed smiling robots on the dance floors of America, robots who then go on to teach the Twinkle-Toes method of dance to their unwary friends and defenseless children."

"That bad?" I asked.

"Worse, far worse," said Astaire as Talbott came back to the table with an overloaded dog and a double side of fries.

"Before you put your teeth into that, Willie," I said,

pulling his full paper plate in front of me the moment he put it on the table. "Tell me what you had on Luna."

Talbott looked to Astaire for help. The dancer was impassive under his Greek fisherman's cap.

"Okay," said Talbott with a sigh, glancing at the two lunching women who were sipping Pepsi and eyeing our table. "I needed a few dollars and I asked for a loan from Luna, just enough to pay off a few debts. You saw back there."

"We saw," Astaire said.

"Well," Talbott went on, "I'm not proud of it, but I told Luna I'd tell Fingers Forbes that she used to work in cheap dime-a-dance joints when she got started and that she was overfriendly with some of the clients when I took her under my tutelage at On Your Toes. All right?"

Talbott reached for his plate. I pushed his hand away.

"You're lying," I said, eating a couple of his fries.

"Me?" Talbott said, putting his left hand to his chest and once again looking at Astaire for help.

"I think Mr. Peters means you've told us a lie of omission," said Astaire. "What you've told us may be true, but it wasn't enough to hold Luna Martin up for blackmail."

I nodded my approval of Astaire's reading of the situation.

Talbott ran his tongue over his lower lip and then nervously chewed at it. I assumed this was an indication of deep thought.

"If I can get back to Seattle, my uncle—his name's Jeff—owns some buildings. He'll take me on as an apprentice janitor, a hundred a week, which is more than I ever made dancing."

"There's something telling in that," said Astaire. "What will it take to get you to Seattle?"

"It's not that I'm not grateful you two came along, but . . . five hundred. That'll keep me going for a while."

I looked at Astaire and thought I saw a go-ahead behind his glasses.

"Three hundred, if the information is good," I said.

Talbott nodded and said, after an elaborate sigh, "She was still seeing someone she met at the studio. After she got together with Forbes. From what Luna said, I think she was still seeing whoever it was right up to now. She said Forbes would definger her if he found out, and she'd be lucky if that was all he did to her. So, I figured when things got a little difficult for me, Luna might come up with enough to get me to Seattle. Is that so bad?"

"It's blackmail," I said. "And I think you're still lying."

Talbott reached for the plate again. I pushed his hand away again.

"Have a heart, here. The food's getting cold."

"Who was she seeing?" I asked.

"Not sure. I've got a guess. But I'm not sure. Look, let's make it five hundred and I give you a list of all of Luna's clients since she came to On Your Toes. Don't worry. It's not a long list."

"Four hundred," Astaire said.

Talbott shrugged his agreement and reached for the plate warily. I let him take it.

"I keep the books in my apartment," said Twinkle-Toes. "Nice and neat. All in a row. Every payment. Every lesson date with a comment by the teacher. Five hundred and the book is yours, plus my best guess on who Luna was still seeing." Talbott stuffed the hot dog in his mouth and took a big bite. His cheek expanded as he chewed and looked at us.

"Five hundred," Astaire said.

The two women had finished their lunch and were advancing cautiously on our table. Astaire turned his head away.

"And we go to your apartment right after you finish eating," I said. "You give us the book and your best guess and we drive you to the bus station."

Talbott nodded.

"Excuse me," said one of the two women, a brunette with swept-up hair, a little hat, and a dark twill suit. Up close she looked more like forty than twenty, but still not bad.

Her younger, blond companion, in a tan dress, hovered behind her.

"Yes," I said.

"Could we have an autograph?" the brunette said.

I looked at Astaire, who nodded.

The woman came up with a pad of paper from her purse and placed it in front of the startled Willie Talbott.

"If you'd just write, 'To Gretchen from her friend Brian Aherne.'"

Talbott took the pad and the fountain pen Gretchen offered and signed.

"Thank you," said the woman with a grin, looking at the autograph and inscription and showing it to her friend, who said, "I thought you spelled your name 'Aherne.'"

"That's my stage and movie spelling," Talbott said. "The traditional family spelling is 'Ahurn' and I promised my mother before she died that I'd always use the family spelling, even in contracts."

"You don't have an English accent?" the blonde said.

"Lost it years ago. Now . . ." Talbott said with a sigh, "I have to fake it. I could tell you about the family history if you're really interested."

The blonde looked at her friend, who encouraged her with a nod.

"Well, I can give you my . . ."

"Remember you're leaving town, Mr. Aherne," I reminded Talbott.

"Right," he said. "Sorry, ladies."

The women nodded their good-byes and walked away, looking at the autograph.

"You don't look anything like Brian Aherne," I said.

"People think I look like Sonny Tufts," said Talbott, finishing the last crumb on his plate and wiping his hands on a paper napkin. "Well, if you've got the five hundred, I'm ready to go home and pack and give you the list."

"The man has *hutzpah*," said Astaire.

"*Chutzpah,*" Talbott corrected. "With a *ch* at the beginning and you make the *ch* sound like you're trying to bring something bad up that you ate for lunch."

"Thanks for the Yiddish lesson," Astaire said, looking at me.

"We can go now, Mr. Aherne," I said.

Talbott searched around for something else to eat, didn't find it, and stood reluctantly. "Two-fifty in advance and the rest in cash when I hand you Luna's schedule and give you my ideas about who to look for?"

"We'll have to stop at my bank," said Astaire, also rising.

Talbott kept talking as Astaire drove and listened to the radio. "Songs by Morton Downey" came on and Raymond Paige's Orchestra played a smooth introduction to "Old Man River" after the announcer told us of the joys of drinking Coca-Cola. I didn't even bother to grunt at the pauses in Talbott's patter. My behind was now a tender red welt that felt every pebble under the tires. Talbott's apartment in Venice was in a three-story pink building about two miles from the Pacific Ocean.

Astaire cruised past the entrance and we scanned the street, looking for the bulldog and the Saint Bernard. There was no sign of them or any other creditors, at least none that Talbott recognized, though he thought the two sailors with a young, overly made-up girl between them looked suspicious.

"Pull in there," Talbott said, pointing to a driveway between two apartment buildings that looked just like the one he lived in.

Astaire pulled in and we went down a narrow concrete path to an open space and three garage doors. "I'll turn the car around," Astaire said.

I nodded, and Talbott leaned forward from the back seat to say, "Look, I know you're damn good, but anyone can learn. Right? So, I'll throw in a couple of special steps I learned at the feet of the great one."

"You'll teach me some dance steps?" Astaire said, looking over his shoulder at Talbott, who nodded.

"Steps I learned from Harvey Burke himself."

"Harvey Burke?"

"Himself," said Talbott, opening the door. "Two-fifty up front. We'll stop at your bank on the way to the bus station."

Astaire pulled out his wallet and came up with, "Two hundred and four."

Talbott took the money and stuffed it into his pocket. "You know Harvey Burke's pancake-and-picture method, right?" he said, looking at Astaire and then at me.

"We'll talk about it later," Astaire said.

Talbott got out of the car and so did I. A throbbing *tuchus* made it tough to keep up with Talbott, who went through a heavy white door and started up a flight of steel steps. We clanked upward in the early-afternoon light that beamed down through a dusty skylight. At the third-floor landing we went through another door and down a corridor past apartments on both sides.

After a right turn we went through a fire-exit door, across a gravel-covered roof, and stepped over the low wall where two buildings pressed against each other. Across this roof and then over another low wall.

"What the hell are we doing, Twinkle-Toes?"

"Making sure," he said as we headed for a steel door on the third roof.

"You come this way a lot?" I asked.

"When skies are cloudy and gray," he said with a confident grin.

I didn't care for this new air of confidence. I followed him down a short flight of stairs and along a corridor. He stopped at an apartment. Down the hall someone was playing Buddy Clark's "Hugo and Igo."

"That's the stairway down," he said softly, gesturing. "Keep an eye and ear on it. Somebody comes, give me a call and we'll get the hell out of here. It'll only take me a couple of minutes."

He went in and closed the door while I waited in the corridor.

Buddy Clark sang on and two minutes passed, or what seemed like two minutes. My old man's watch on my wrist seemed to indicate that time had gone backwards.

I tried the handle of Talbott's apartment. It was open.

The place was a mess. Twinkle-Toes may have been a lousy housekeeper but this was abusing the privilege. Someone had been through the place, tossed and turned it.

"Willie," I called, stepping over a faded tan pillow that had been thrown from the sofa against the wall.

No answer.

The place wasn't big. Living room, kitchen combination, and what looked like a bedroom on the left. The door was closed. I avoided a purple table lamp on the floor. The lamp had lost its shade. I turned and picked up the lamp. I didn't know if I would need a weapon.

I opened the door and looked into Talbott's bedroom, a horror of seduction-purple velvet and dirty white. The bedding and mattress had been ripped to shreds. My lamp and I went to the closed door beyond the bed. I tripped on a small radio but kept my balance. I pushed open the door and found a small empty bathroom. The window over the tub was open. I went for it and heard a shot. There was a narrow space between Talbott's apartment building and the next one. I could imagine Talbott, who knew the best ways in and out, inching his way to the windowsill and then reaching up to the roof and pulling himself up. There was no way I could make it through that space, even if I were thirty and didn't have a sore ass.

I could hear footsteps on the gravel of the next roof. I dropped the lamp and hurtled through the maze of bad taste that littered the floor. I ran down the corridor and up to the roof the way we had come. I looked to my left, saw nothing, and then looked right, where Talbott lay sprawled facedown on the next roof, his left knee bent, his right hand over his head as if he were about to demonstrate one of those steps he had promised Astaire. There was nobody else in sight, but the door to the roof a few feet from Talbott was open.

The space between the two buildings was only a couple of feet. I climbed on the wall and jumped and tumbled, rolling over on my right shoulder and tearing my poplin jacket.

I ran to the edge of the roof at the rear of the building and leaned over. A small space between garages. No people. I ran to the front of the building. Someone was getting into a dark car right below me. The car was parked in front of a fire plug. I didn't see the face of the person getting in the car, but I did see his or her gloved hand. It was clutching what looked like a leatherbound ledger book. The car door closed with a slam and the driver screeched out of the space and down the street.

Talbott wasn't moving. I got down on one knee and turned him over.

The hole in his shirt was black and the blood that stained

his chest was thick. No doubts here—Willie Talbott was dead. I went back over the roofs and followed the trail Talbott had taken to get to his apartment.

In the garage turn-around Astaire was leaning back on the front fender of his car, his arms folded. He stood up, looked beyond me, and saw no Twinkle-Toes.

"I thought I heard a shot," he said.

"Talbott's danced his last bad samba," I said. "He's dead and I think the killer got away with Luna's appointment book. Let's go."

"Where?" he asked, opening the door.

"To my car," I said, going around the hood and heading for the passenger side.

We got in and closed the doors. Astaire started down the narrow driveway.

"Needless to say, I have some questions, Peters," Astaire said, turning right when we hit the street. Behind us a small gathering of neighbors on the sidewalk looked up at the building where Talbott lay dead. One of them was pointing.

"I probably don't have very good answers. I'll take my car, go to the cops, tell them what happened. I'll leave you out of it. You've got nothing to tell them that I can't. The way I figure it, Talbott got the appointment book and went out the bathroom window. I think he figured that if he could get five hundred from you, he might be able to get a lot more from someone whose name was in that book. That someone was waiting for Talbott on the roof, was familiar with Talbott's exits, shot him, took the book. Of course, I could have it all wrong and the bulldog and Saint Bernard you took apart just caught up with him and were in a bad mood, but they didn't know about the appointment book, at least I think they didn't."

"So? . . ." asked Astaire.

"We've got two dead dancers," I said. "And no idea who killed either one of them."

"I'm going with you to the police," Astaire said as we headed back toward Los Angeles.

"What'll it get you? Some very bad publicity? Who is it going to help? I'll tell you what. Give me a couple of days and if the police or I don't turn anything up, I'll set up a meeting between you and a homicide detective. Three days."

"You said 'a couple.' That's two."

"Okay, two days. Then you can go to the police and ruin your career."

He drove me to my car around the corner from the now-ownerless On Your Toes Dance Studio and I headed for the Wilshire Police Station, which was a long way from Venice. My behind was sore. My stomach was upset. I'd lost a witness and let the killer get away. My jacket was torn and my ex-wife was marrying a movie star. I took off the jacket and placed it on the passenger seat. Exhibit A. I was not having a good day.

I parked behind the Wilshire station in a spot reserved for patrol cars and went through the rear door, passing a pair of uniformed police, one too old, the other too young. A wartime phenomenon.

"Russ," I said to the older cop. "How are things?"

Russ paused, and his young partner, who I didn't know, looked impatiently at his watch.

"Remember my kid, Charlie? You met him at Sonny's bar a couple or so times?" Russ asked.

"Sure I remember him."

"Just got back home. Wounded, but safe. Arm won't move great." Russ demonstrated how his son's arm would be moving. "But what the hell. He's back in one piece and for good with a Purple Heart."

"That's great," I said.

"Russ," the young partner said.

"Right," Russ said. "Gotta go, Toby. Say, you know what's gnawing at Phil? He's got a bug up his ass the size of Tarzana."

"No," I said, and Russ and his partner headed for their car.

I went down the damp, dimly lit corridor, past the downstairs meeting and interrogation rooms and up the badly worn stairs. Then past the squad room, where shrill nervous voices and deep bored ones came through the closed double doors along with the smell of stale food. My brother was back in his old office at the end of the squad room. When he had been promoted to captain, he had moved into an ugly brown square across from the squad room. The captain's office would have been enough to drive a monk nuts. He had gone back to his closet-sized office after his demotion for failure to deal effectively with the local business people. He seemed to be happier back with the boys, though it was hard to tell when Phil was happy. I couldn't remember ever seeing him smile.

The squad room was busy. A thin kid who needed a shave was seated next to Jay Buxbaum. The kid was probably Mexican. He had an accent. He was pointing to his own chest and saying, "You really saying I did this thing? That what you're saying?"

"That's what I'm saying," said Buxbaum, evenly settling his three hundred pounds back in his chair.

At another desk near the window, two detectives, Winslow and Ho, were leaning over a pale man. They were whispering. The pale man was shaking his head. I nodded at a detective named Ponsetto and made my way to Phil's office. I knocked and he said, "All right."

I took that for a "come in."

Phil had his back turned to me and was looking out the

window. Phil never took the time to look out windows. There were too many criminals out there who needed a good hit in the head and there was too little time to get to them all. Besides, the view from Phil's window was a brick wall five feet away.

I stood in front of his desk. He didn't turn to face me but he did say, "Sit down."

I would have preferred to stand, but I didn't want to remind him that I had been spanked by a giant Indian. I sat. Phil continued to look out the window for about two minutes. Then he sighed and swiveled in his wooden chair to face me. He put his hands on his desk and looked at me.

Phil was nearing two hundred and fifty pounds. His hair was gray and getting whiter by the week. His neck was thick and his collar was open, the blue tie dangling awkwardly down his shirt.

"You okay, Phil?"

He looked at me without blinking.

"Phil?"

"I like my work," he said. "I didn't like being a captain. But where you've got a vacuum, it has to be filled."

"Have you been drinking, Phil?"

"No," he said. "But I'll probably have a couple of beers when I get home. The vacuum is the captaincy. It's been filled by the all-damn-knowing chief of police. Do you know who the new captain of the Wilshire is? You want to guess?"

"No," I said.

"Guess," Phil insisted.

"Perkily from the Hollywood," I tried.

Phil shook his head. I tried to think. I came up with six more names, all of which got me the same response.

"Claudette Colbert," I said.

Phil held up a hand to show that he was not to be trifled with.

"I give up," I said. "I mean, I'm enjoying the game but I've got something I've got to talk to you about."

"Cawelti," he said. "That son of a bitch on the take is my boss."

John Cawelti, he of the plastered-back, bartender-combed red hair and bad complexion, had, when the chance came, tried to nail me for everything from stealing the collection money at St. Vincent De Paul's to murder. John Cawelti and I had a long and rotten history.

"Shit," I said.

"I've asked for a transfer. I don't think they'll give it to me. Steve's asked for one too. He might get his. I can retire early, but . . ." He let it trail off and sighed. "Okay, Toby, what do you want?"

"Something that'll make you look good," I said. "A third-rate dance teacher named Willie Talbott was shot on an apartment roof in Venice a little over an hour ago. Luna Martin used to work for him at the On Your Toes Dance Studio. Someone tossed Talbott's room looking for something. I'd say the two murders might be connected."

Phil grunted.

"In fact," I went on. "I'm sure they're related."

I told Phil the story about my going to the studio, finding Talbott, making the deal for Luna's appointment schedule, and then going with Talbott to his apartment and missing his murder. I left out the part about Fred Astaire being with me. Phil grunted, pulled a pad of paper out of his desk drawer, which was no mean feat since there was nowhere for Phil to back up to have enough room to open the drawer more than a few inches. Phil took some notes and looked up at me.

He pursed his lips, stared at me, and hummed a few bars of what sounded like "Tiger Rag." Then he looked down at his pad and said, "You interfered with a murder investigation by not going to the police as soon as you knew about this appointment book. You left the scene of a murder though you were the only witness. You've been present at two murders in one day."

"I really didn't see . . ."

"I know that, Tobias. That's your problem."

My real name is Tobias Leon Pevsner. Toby Peters is my professional name. Philip Martin Pevsner does not approve of his brother dropping the family name. Phil doesn't approve of a lot of things, but this one is a favorite.

"Find Steve out there," Phil said, waving his hand toward the noisy squad room. "He'll take your statement."

We sat silently. Phil turned back toward the window and put his hands behind his head, his thick fingers locking. I got up.

"Maybe you'd feel better if you just threw something at me, Phil. You know, like the good old days."

"Get out," he said.

"Look . . ."

"Out," Phil repeated.

I got out, found Steve Seidman. He was walking toward his desk in the corner near the window. He looked even more pale and thin than he had that morning.

"I've got a statement, Steve. Phil said I should see you."

Seidman got behind his desk and motioned me into the battered wooden chair next to it.

"Mind if I stand?" I said.

"Suit yourself."

The Mexican kid started to yell. "He thinks I stabbed Jorge," he screamed above the noise of the squad room. "I din' stab Jorge. I don' know who stabbed Jorge, but it wasn't fuckin' me."

Buxbaum just sat playing with a rubber band. No one

paid any attention to the Mexican kid. I gave my statement to Seidman, who typed it up as I stood there.

"Phil tell you Cawelti's on top?"

"He told me."

"Politics," Seidman said, hitting the keys of the Remington.

The kid was yelling louder now. The squad room doors opened and Cawelti stepped in in a new blue suit.

"Shut him up," Cawelti shouted, pointing at the kid.

The room went silent except for the kid, who was now talking Spanish. Buxbaum nodded, put down his rubber band, and stood up with a grunt. The kid kept screaming; he turned to Cawelti and called him a series of colorful names. Cawelti's pocked face turned nearly as red as his hair.

"Bring this piece of crap to my office, Buxbaum. Fast."

Buxbaum grabbed the kid's left arm. The kid pulled away. Cawelti shot forward, punched the kid in the stomach, kneed him in the groin, and hit him square on the nose with his right elbow. The kid went down and said no more.

"Add resisting arrest to whatever else you've got on him," Cawelti said, adjusting his jacket and taking a step toward the door.

Then, sensing additional prey, he turned and scanned the room, almost missing me in the corner. Our eyes met and Cawelti gave me a smile I did not like. I returned the smile and he strode across the room toward me. The room was still silent.

Cawelti and I were face to face.

"If you're not a witness or, better yet, a suspect, get your ass out of here," he said. "I don't want to see you in here."

"Witness," Seidman said, pointing at his report.

Cawelti's face and mine were no more than six inches apart now.

"To what?"

"Murder," Seidman said.

Cawelti's smile broadened. It really was one awful-looking smile. I dug in my pocket and came up with a packet of Sen-Sen. I handed it to him. He threw it on the wooden floor.

"I want that report on my desk in the next fifteen minutes."

Seidman nodded.

"Congratulations on your promotion," I said. "I'm sure you and the local merchants will get along just fine."

"Soon," Cawelti said, pointing a finger at my nose. "We'll meet soon."

He turned, crossed the squad room, nodded at Buxbaum to bring the bleeding and bent-over kid, and went out. The noise level began to climb.

"Can I go, Steve?"

"Go," Seidman said. "We'll get back to you if we need you."

I moved past Buxbaum, who was keeping the kid from falling over.

"What'd I do?" the kid said through the blood leaking from his nose. "What'd I do?"

"Exercised your right to free speech," Buxbaum said.

I escaped into the corridor, went quickly past Cawelti's office, the office that used to be my brother's, and got down to my Crosley. I eased into my seat on top of Mrs. Plaut's pillow.

My guess was that it was close to five. I turned on the radio as I drove, waiting for the time. The news guy told me that Trygvie Lie, the foreign minister of the Norwegian Government in Exile, was sure the Norwegians would welcome an Allied invasion of Norway. I then found out that Anthony Eden was in Washington to talk about postwar issues and J. P. Morgan had died at the age of seventy-five of a heart attack. At the end of the news, a happy woman sang, "It's five o'clock. Gruen watch time. Ticktock."

I headed for the Monticello Hotel. I had things to discuss with Arthur Forbes.

Chapter Eight

First You Put Your Two Knees Close Up Tight

When I got to the Monticello, I realized I should have called first. The desk clerk, a thin guy with a funeral-director smile and a blue-serge suit, told me he was sorry but Mr. Forbes and Mrs. Forbes were not in the hotel. He assumed, but he wasn't sure, that they had gone home.

"I thought he lived here," I said. "When do you expect him back?"

"Who knows? Mr. Forbes has many business enterprises and social obligations," the clerk said, leaning over to copy something from one open book to another.

"Where might Mr. Forbes live?" I asked, flashing my own unwinning grin.

"I do not know Mr. Forbes's address, and if I did know I'm afraid I wouldn't be at liberty to give you the information. You might try the telephone directory," he said, still leaning over his busy work. "But . . ."

"Unlisted."

"Unlisted. You could leave a message."

A nervous blond young man in tan slacks, his white shirt open at the collar, jangled across the lobby with his hands in his pockets.

"Change for a hundred," he said, reaching into his pocket and pulling out a crinkled bill.

The clerk nodded, opened the cash drawer, and took the bill. The nervous guy eyed me and turned to get his money. He counted it and moved away.

"I work for Mr. Forbes," I said to the clerk.

"Who doesn't?" answered the clerk, closing two books in front of him and looking up at me.

"You've got a point. Listen, I need a break here," I whispered, reaching for my wallet. "I'm a private detective. I've been hired to investigate the murder of Luna Martin."

The clerk waved my hand away before I even got the wallet out of my back pocket.

"You have nothing in that billfold that would overcome my fear of what Mr. Forbes might say or do to me were he to find out I gave you his address."

"Then you do know it," I said.

The clerk sighed, pursed his lips, and looked across the lobby at the hotel doors, which had just opened to an arguing couple. The man looked like he was in his late forties. The woman was under thirty and properly round.

"Good evening, Mr. Hooper," the clerk said.

Mr. Hooper, in a white suit and a bad mood, waved and kept walking.

"Claims to be a movie producer," the clerk confided, leaning toward me. "Car dealer from Chicago. That's his secretary. Wife's back home fighting the wind and watching the kids."

"You're sharing this information with me for a reason or you just want to be pals?"

"I'm a born gossip," the clerk said. "Probably why I'm still a desk clerk and not on my way up the ladder at Paramount. I liked Miss Martin. She was tough, knew what she wanted, and always had a good word and a few minutes for me and the bellhops. You hang around Mr. Forbes and his friends and bad things are bound to happen."

"Ever trade gossip with Luna Martin?"

"That," he said with a smile, "I can sell."

My wallet came out again. I pulled out two tens and handed them to the clerk, who glanced around to be sure no one was watching. He handed one back to me and stuffed the other into his pocket.

"Too much," he said. "I don't have that much to sell. Luna thought Mrs. Forbes was well aware of her existence and her relationship to Mrs. Forbes's husband."

"Was she?"

"Is Lincoln dead? Luna was putting pressure on Mr. Forbes to divorce the missus and marry her," the clerk said.

"She confided all this to you?" I asked.

"I'm easy to talk to," the clerk said. "You want to listen or you want to talk?"

"I'll listen," I said.

"I think Luna gave him a time limit, but I don't know what it was. Anyway, I'm sure Mr. Forbes had no intention of divorcing his wife and marrying Luna. Mrs. Forbes is the daughter of Guiseppi Cortona. Mr. Cortona is very much alive, very fond of his daughter, and very much in charge of Minneapolis."

"She told you this?"

"I stand behind here playing with keys, sorting mail, writing in ledgers, and listening to people who stand five feet away from this desk and talk softly in the mistaken belief that the desk makes them invisible and me deaf."

"Got you," I said. "Anything else?"

He shook his head.

"Slow night," I said, surveying the empty lobby.

"Tomorrow morning will be hell and a half," he said, looking around as if he were seeing the hordes of dawn. "When the newspapers hit the streets tonight, the ghouls will suddenly decide that a weekend at the Monticello might be fun. You know, a peek at the ballroom and the lobby, maybe a glimpse of Mr. Forbes. Mostly would-be writers who see a quick script. You know."

"It's happened before?"

The clerk shrugged. "A former business associate of Mr. Forbes's from Detroit was the unfortunate victim of a robbery in the elevator the week Mr. Forbes took possession of the then St. Lawrence. The former associate was a Mr. Seymour Bratz, also known as Rat-tat-tat Bratz. The elevator came down." He nodded at the elevator. "The door opened and Mr. Bratz was sitting inside alone and very dead."

"You saw it?"

"Though I didn't note at the time that the robber had taken the time between the eighth and ground floors to remove two of Mr. Bratz's fingers. These two."

The clerk put up his right hand and held up the pinkie and the finger next to it.

"The ghouls came?"

"Descended," the clerk said with a nod.

"So it doesn't get boring behind the Monticello desk."

"It beats being shot at by the Japs," he said. "My two younger brothers are both having that pleasant experience. My older brother was killed on Guadalcanal."

"Sorry," I said.

"Well, I got the waiver. Mother insisted. I was considered to be the weak one and a bit . . ."

"Sensitive."

"Let's call it 'fey,'" he said.

"You tell your life story to everyone?"

"Just the ones who pay ten bucks for it. You've got a phone call."

"What?"

"The lobby phone. Over there."

There were two phones sitting on a table with a dark marble top. The table was about a dozen feet away against a wall. The phones weren't ringing and the clerk hadn't spoken to anyone.

"I don't . . ."

"I do," he said, cocking his head to one side while I took a beat to figure out the situation. I moved to the phones and picked one up. Nothing. I picked up the other one.

"Mr. Peters?"

I looked back at the desk. The clerk wasn't there.

"Yes."

"Forty-seven Mountain Top Road, Huntington Beach."

The line went dead. I hung up the phone and looked over at the desk, where the clerk was just moving back behind it, a stack of papers in his hands. I nodded to him, but he didn't look up.

I went through the front doors and into a threat of rain.

Cotton Wright, the parking-lot attendant, was seated on a low wooden stool, trying to make sense out of a crumpled issue of the *L.A. Times*.

"Yes," he said, looking up at me.

"My car."

"Your . . ."

"This is the parking lot," I said. "And that little Crosley back in the corner is mine."

"I know," said Cotton, standing up and touching his scalp through his thin hair.

"Your head humming?"

"Yeah," he said. "Did I tell you about that?"

I nodded.

"Sometimes I get the wars confused," he said, heading for the Crosley past a wide array of vehicles that made my car look like a tiny battered rolling refrigerator, which it was.

Whatever else was Cotton's problem, he could drive. He eased the Crosley out of a tight space that wasn't really a space, and pulled the car smoothly to my side.

"Little," he said, getting out.

"Cheap," I said, handing him four quarters and getting into the car and on top of my borrowed pillow.

"Someone asked me once if I could hear the radio through the plate in my head," he said, leaning down to talk to me through the open window.

"Can you?"

"No," he said. "That don't make any sense. My plate hums."

"Proud of that plate, aren't you, Cotton?" I asked with a smile.

"Earned it," he said, seriously.

The Farraday was about ten minutes from the Monticello and on the way to Huntington Beach, if you've got an active imagination and a very sore ass. It was almost six. Main Street was just waking up from its afternoon nap. There were a few parking spaces.

Knowing where to park in Los Angeles was about as tough as figuring out food-ration stamps. Mrs. Plaut was the food-ration expert. I knew parking. No parking along red or yellow curb. Three-minute limit at white curb. Fifteen-minute limit at a green curb, otherwise forty-five-minute parking in the Central Traffic District from 7:00 A.M. to 4:30 P.M. No parking from 4:30 to 6:00 P.M. And unlimited parking from 6:00 P.M. to 2:00 A.M., thirty-minute parking from 2:00 A.M. to 4:00 A.M., and unlimited parking from 4:00 to 7:00 A.M.

I parked about half a block from the Farraday, eased out of the Crosley, and headed down the street past trios and quartets of uniformed soldiers and sailors, some of them with smiling young and not-so-young women. A pair of Latin zoot-suiters were leaning against the wall to the right of the entrance to the Farraday. They were talking earnestly to Juanita the seer, who had an office on the fifth floor just below mine and Shelly's.

Juanita is a bejangled psychic with a few years behind her. She wore clothes that Carmen Miranda would find too flamboyant, but she disdained turbans. Juanita had lost a husband back in New Jersey. I think he died. Or, she might simply have misplaced him on the subway. "Alex could still be riding up and down to Coney for all I know," Juanita had once said to me, fingering a silver earring the size and shape of Baja California.

Juanita had discovered her powers early and given in to them only after two husbands and a quarter of a century as a housewife. Juanita was good at reading tea leaves, coffee grounds, toenails, the palm of your hand, and the top of your head. "All show," she had confided to me once in a whisper. "It either comes to me in a flash, like that, or nothing. But clients like a show. This is Los Angeles, right?"

Since it was, I had nodded.

The problem with Juanita's insights was that you couldn't really figure out what they meant till it was too late.

I tried to step past Juanita and the two Mexicans.

"Pain," she suddenly said, turning to me. "You're in pain."

"How you doing, Juanita?" I said.

Juanita was painted for Indian wars or serious seeing into the future. Her mouth was as red as a stoplight and her eyebrows as dark as tomorrow. Her perfume was as sweet and heavy as a Chunky candy bar. I glanced at the zoot suits. They looked me up and down and weren't impressed.

"I'm doin' great, Tobe, but you've got a pain. Not the knees."

"His ass," one of the zoot-suiters said.

"He a seer too?" I asked.

"No, man," the zoot-suiter said. "I just see the way you walking. Like when I was a kid and my old man whooped me with a stick."

"Your ass hurts, Toby?" Juanita said softly, with some concern.

"You asking or telling?"

"Both," she said. "This is Vic and José. They're brothers. They come to me. I tell them stuff. They give me stuff. Barter. It's coming back as a means of exchange."

"We got to get going," one of the brothers said impatiently.

"Then you should have come on time," said Juanita, her back to him. "Besides, you don't have any place to go. Your evening and the night are uncharted, though there is a woman named, I think . . ."

"Forget it," the Mexican said nervously. "We're goin'. We'll see you soon, Juanita."

The brothers adjusted their wide-brimmed hats, looked at my less-than–Cary Grant clothes, and departed. Juanita didn't turn to watch them go.

"I've got to get going," I said.

She took my right hand and looked into my eyes. "You've been dancin'?" she asked.

"Question?"

"No," she said. "You've been dancin'. I used to dance when I was married to Alex. Nothing fancy. A few steps. I liked it. Alex was a good dancer, if you can imagine that."

Not having known Alex, I could not imagine it.

"More death, Tobe," she said, squeezing my hand and shaking her head. "Dancers are dead. That make sense to you?"

"Yeah," I said. "I've really got to go, Juanita."

"Watch the fourth dancer," she said. "The third dancer is

fire and death. Victim and killer. The fourth dancer is the one you're looking for."

"Juanita, I don't want to know any more."

"I can't stop," she said as a couple passed us. The young man was in civilian clothes. The woman was a WAC. They tried not to look at us in the doorway of the Farraday but we were a compelling sight.

"My curse," Juanita said. "Can't stop telling people their future. You should know that by now. How'd you break your car window?"

"It's not broken," I said.

"Forget it," she said, giving me a smile and a playful punch in the arm. "I think I've got something you'll like. A woman from your past will come to you, a woman of beauty. There was a rejection in the past but she will bring hope to the future."

"Anne?" I said.

"Anne?"

"My former wife. She's supposed to marry Preston Stewart."

"The actor?" Juanita said.

"How many Preston Stewarts can there be?"

"In Hollywood, dozens," she said.

"So, they won't get married?" I asked, feeling like an idiot.

"How should I know?" she said with a jangling shrug.

"How should . . . forget it. I've got to get going."

"Suit yourself," Juanita said, letting my hand go. "See Jeremy."

"I was going to."

"Good," she said, looking down the street. "I'm going. Cass Daley's on the 'Bing Crosby Music Hall' tonight. John Scott Trotter and his orchestra are going to do a patriotic medley. I'm a sucker for that kind of stuff."

And she was gone.

The inner lobby door of the Farraday was locked. A sign over the panel of office names said, "After 6:00 P.M. please call the person you are here to see on the phone. They will come down and let you in."

The sign was part of Jeremy's patient and never-ending struggle against the walking wounded and winos looking for a corner to curl up in for the night. It was tough to come running down five or six flights to let in a client, and some of the tenants who worked late had taken to taping the inner door open which, since the telephone was constantly being stolen, was probably not a bad idea.

Tonight, the inner door was locked.

I used my key, went in, and listened to my footsteps echo across the tiled inner lobby. I liked the sound and the lingering smell of Lysol. The Farraday was evening silent. The dim shadowy night-lights were on. The baby photographer had probably folded his tripod and headed to what he called home. The talent agent on three had dropped his stack of photos of the untalented and unwary into his ragged briefcase and headed across Main for a round or ten of drinks. If any of the tenants remained, I couldn't hear them.

I moved past the iron bars of the unpredictable elevator and started to climb the stairs.

"Toby?"

I looked up seven flights. Jeremy Butler was standing at the railing in front of his apartment, the only apartment in the building.

"It's me, Jeremy," I said, continuing to climb and wondering whether I should have taken a chance on the elevator from hell. Stairs were not a good idea for my sensitive rear.

"I heard the door open," he said.

"I was coming to see you," I said, pulling myself up by the railing.

"You are hurt?"

"You've got it," I said, halfway up the second floor. "Remember that stuff you used on my back, the stuff you used when you were wrestling?"

"Of course."

"Think that'll help a sore rear end?"

"Yes," Jeremy said. "Take the elevator."

I took his advice and pressed the elevator button on the second floor. Two decades later the elevator arrived. I pulled back the grille and took the scenic century-long ride up to the eighth floor. From the elevator I could see as we passed the sixth floor that the lights to Shelly's and my office were out.

When I finally reached the eighth floor and opened the grille, Jeremy had gone back into his apartment. His door was ajar. I followed the light and knocked.

"Come in," Jeremy said. "Alice took Natasha to her cousin's in Monterey for a few days."

Jeremy stood massive, bald, and wearing black slacks, shoes, and a turtleneck sweater. In his hand was a large green bottle of a clear liquid. The room, which had once been the office of a doctor named Hamarion, who proved to have no license, was big and served as living room and office for Jeremy. He had put a door in the walls on either side and used the adjoining offices for a kitchen–dining room and a pair of bedrooms. It was well-ordered, comfortable. In a big open box near the window, Natasha's toys overflowed.

"Take off your pants and lean over," he said.

I closed the door behind me and moved to Jeremy's desk near the window. I dropped my pants and underpants and leaned over.

"This was done by Kudlap Singh?" he asked.

"The Beast of Bombay," I confirmed.

Then a cold liquid sensation washed through me, from my

sore behind to the tips of my fingers. It didn't hurt exactly, but I couldn't say that it felt great.

"Give it a moment before you put your pants back on," he said. "And don't sit yet."

I turned, still tingling, and faced Jeremy.

"There is a poetic irony here," Jeremy said, putting the cap back on the bottle. "I learned of this treatment from Kudlap Singh. The year was 1930. The Memorial Auditorium in Sacramento a few years after it opened. We were the main event. It was his turn to win. I suffered a sprain in my right thigh when I did an airplane spin."

"You hoisted Kudlap Singh over your head?"

Jeremy nodded.

"And he used this on me and told me how to get more from an Indian apothecary in Kansas City."

"Can I pull my pants up now?"

"Yes."

I pulled my underpants up slowly. I can't say the pain was completely gone, but it was certainly almost asleep.

"I think it worked," I said as Jeremy put the bottle on his desk.

"It has remarkable anesthetic qualities," he said. "Take the bottle. Return it when you've recovered. It should only be a day or so."

I pulled my pants up, took the bottle, and thanked him.

I tested my new freedom from agony by sitting in Jeremy's wooden desk chair. It wasn't bad.

"I was just writing a poem," Jeremy said, reaching behind me and picking up a pad of paper. "Would you be interested in hearing it?"

"Yes, I would."

"Stephen Vincent Benét died in New York early today," Jeremy said. "He was only forty-four."

"Sorry," I said.

"You know who he was?"

"Poet," I said.

"When I was still perspiring in wrestling rings from Seattle to Miami, that twenty-nine-year-old genius had written 'John Brown's Body,' more than one hundred thousand words in a single poem, and he had won the Pulitzer Prize."

Such enthusiasm was rare in Jeremy so I kept my mouth shut and listened.

"Have you read 'The Devil and Daniel Webster'?" he asked.

"Don't think so," I said.

"I've got copies in two anthologies. I'll let you read it and 'John Brown's Body.'"

"Thanks," I said, savoring my relative freedom from pain.

"The poem," Jeremy said, looking down at the pad in his hand as he stood in front of me.

> John Brown's body lies a moldering in the grave
> joined by poet, freeman and ghostly slave.
> What can one say
> of Stephen Vincent Benét?
> He came, was struck by fevered urge
> to pen his genius in a massive dirge.
> Meteor burned young on entering the uncertain air
> of earth, burned and took his talent rare
> to the far reaches of time
> where he will soar and rhyme
> and carry on conversations that through Heaven re-
> sound
> with Daniel Webster and old John Brown.

Jeremy looked down at me over the top of his pad.

"Resound and Brown do not rhyme," he said. "I'm not sure whether I should find something to rhyme with Webster and switch the names or live with the closing with a slant rhyme. Your feelings?"

"Sounds great to me the way it is," I said. "What rhymes with Webster?"

"I'm inclined to leave it as it is," Jeremy said, reaching past me to lay his pad on the desk.

I got up, tested my tingle, and pronounced myself almost cured.

"More irony for you, Jeremy," I said. "I'm probably going to see your old friend Kudlap Singh in less than an hour."

"Is the situation such that he might inflict further pain on you?"

"It is a distinct possibility," I said, testing my powers by walking across the Persian rug covering most of the wooden floor.

"My poem is finished. I think I'd like to accompany you, if you have no objection."

"It could be uncomfortable," I said. "I'm going to see Kudlap's boss, who has been known to remove the fingers of those who he finds annoying."

"An odd and phallic fetish," Jeremy said.

"You're telling me," I said. "I promised Alice I wouldn't put you in danger again."

Jeremy folded his arms and looked at me without a smile. Jeremy had no smiles except for his wife and daughter and no frowns except for the endless parade of men without a place to sleep who sought out the corners of the Farraday.

"If you hide from every possible danger," he said, "you find yourself discovering more and more dangers until you hide from everyone and everything. If you confront danger and your fears, you either overcome them and respect yourself or you are destroyed and die with dignity."

I didn't buy it but I knew I'd feel more comfortable with

Jeremy at my side if Forbes decided to have the Beast of Bombay rip off one of my legs or a few of my fingers.

"I'm not asking you, Jeremy," I said. "If you tell Alice about this . . ."

"I tell Alice of all my significant actions and thoughts."

"She is very likely to throw me over the railing out there," I said, pointing to the door. "I'll make a splash that Lysol will never get rid of."

"Is it a cool night?" he asked.

"Getting there," I said. "Looks like rain."

He went into the bedroom and returned with a light jacket, also black.

We stopped at my office and found a note from Violet hanging from a thumbtack on my door. It said I had received two calls from an Anita Maloney. Anita had left her number. The message concluded with, "Bivins won a split over Mauriello, in case you missed it. Heard it on the radio. Barney Ross was there. Announcer said his hair was gray and he was limping. Hope my husband doesn't come back like that. You can pay me in the morning."

I folded Violet's message and put it in my shirt pocket.

There was no way, outside of major tutoring from Emmett Kelly, that Jeremy Butler could fit in my Crosley. We took his car, a five-year-old dark Buick.

"Juanita trapped me in front of the building a little while ago," I said. "Said something about a third dancer and a woman from the past."

"Juanita is in tune with the universal oneness," Jeremy said, weaving through traffic. "Her curse is that she is inevitably right but so obscure that one cannot heed her advice and warnings. A modern Cassandra."

We used my ration card to fill the tank at a Sinclair station on Melrose and then we stopped for a quick dinner at a restaurant Jeremy knew. We ate things that were green and brown and good for you and tasted terrible. And then we were on our way.

I asked Jeremy if it was all right if I played the radio. It was his car. He said yes. We listened to the last fifteen minutes of "Stage Door Canteen." Bert Lytell and George Jessel were trying to explain the rationing system to Billie Burke, who was as bewildered as Gracie Allen. After they failed, Lawrence Tibbett sang an aria from *La Traviata.*

For the rest of the trip we listened to a classical music station that kept fading out until it was a distant scratch.

Before the war there were less than three thousand people in Huntington Beach and an oil derrick or two, but the handful of bleak derricks had been joined by dozens and dozens of others as the wartime need for fuel had increased. People to work the rigs and tend them and the people who sold things to the people who worked the rigs moved in. Huntington Beach was a boom town.

The tidelands of Huntington Beach were state property, but oil operators had found a new technique of drilling to bypass the state's rights. From the town lots they had quietly and cheaply purchased, they drilled on a bias to tap the oil pools under the tidelands. In 1929 Governor Culbert L. Olson had tried to put through a bill to permit the state of California to control the oil operators and tap the oil pools for state profit. The oil lobby beat the governor in court and the whole thing was pushed aside by the rush of fear that followed Pearl Harbor.

And so Huntington Beach became a mess of pumping dark steel, and the sun-worshippers and tourists moved on to Newport Beach and Long Beach.

We found Arthur Forbes's house just before the sun went down. It was on a street of big old wooden houses on a hill overlooking the sea and the derricks. It had once been a hell of a view. We parked in the driveway behind another car, one

I recognized. Forbes's car was probably tucked in the garage. It was a modest driveway but an impressive house with polished marble steps leading up to the door. There were lights on and the distant sound of music inside. I pushed the door bell and heard a chime inside the house.

I looked at Jeremy. He stood with his hands at his sides, showing nothing on his face. On the beach below us, the oil derricks chugged noisily.

The door opened.

A woman wearing black tights opened the door and said, "What the hell do you want?"

"We have business with your husband."

She put her hands on her hips and considered us for a beat or two. Then she slammed the door in our faces.

Chapter Nine

Say, Have You Seen the Carioca?

Jeremy and I looked at each other for a second or two and then I pushed the button again and listened to the chime.

When the door opened this time, Kudlap Singh filled it, blocking out the hallway light. He ignored me and looked at Jeremy as impassively as Jeremy looked at him.

"Mr. Forbes is busy," he said.

"Singh," Jeremy said.

I had to stop myself from putting my hands behind me to protect my rapidly improving rump.

"Mr. Forbes is busy," Singh repeated, looking at me.

"A man that abandons a friend who has learned with him no longer has a share in speech," Jeremy said. "What he does hear he hears in vain, for he does not know the path of good action."

Singh didn't turn his head but his eyes shifted to Jeremy, who looked back at him and continued, "Unkindly I desert him who was kind to me, as I go from my own friends to a foreign tribe."

"A moment, Jeremy Butler," Singh said softly, and the door closed on us again.

"What the hell was that?" I asked.

"Quotations from the *Rig Veda,* an ancient Hindu collection of over a thousand hymns. I've read only a weak British translation from the Sanskrit, but when we were traveling the circuit Singh translated passages for me. The Veda has been a great influence on my poetry and my life."

The derricks pounded on their steel stalks. We waited. The door opened again. Again Kudlap Singh blocked the light.

"Come in," he said, stepping back so we could enter.

We went in. The house was a lot more modest than Fingers Intaglia's wealth and reputation would suggest. Kudlap Singh led the way down a carpeted hallway with paintings of the same man in a powdered wig. I looked at Jeremy, who said, "Thomas Jefferson."

It made a crazy kind of sense. Singh stopped in front of two big wooden doors and knocked.

"Come in," Forbes called.

Singh opened the doors and we stepped in with him. We were in what must have been a big dining room or a library, but it wasn't anymore. One wall was mirrored top to bottom and all the way across. The floors were polished wood. In one corner was a small upright piano. Against one wall were four blue upholstered chairs and a pair of tables, on one of which sat a phonograph. Arthur Forbes in a gray sweat suit was sitting in one of the chairs, wiping himself with a towel. In front of the mirror, her back turned to us, was Carlotta Forbes. She glanced at us in the mirror and then did a series of knee bends.

Standing next to the phonograph was Fred Astaire, sleeves rolled up, red handkerchief around his neck.

"What do you want and who's that?" Forbes asked, continuing to dry himself.

"Yo soy Jeremy Butler, un amigo de Señor Peters," said Jeremy.

"Está bien, pero por qué vienen a mi casa ahora?" Forbes replied. "How did you know I speak Spanish?"

"Thomas Jefferson, whom apparently we both admire,

spoke fluent Spanish and believed that all Americans should."

" 'I hope to see a cordial fraternization among all the American nations—' " Forbes said with a challenge in his voice.

" '—and their coalescing in an American system of policy,' " Jeremy finished.

"You a history professor?" Forbes asked.

"A poet," answered Jeremy.

"A poet," Forbes said with a smile, looking at his wife who ignored him and continued to do knee bends, and then at Fred Astaire who sighed, folded his arms, and leaned against the wall. "You're Battering Butler, the Human Cannonball. I saw you wrestle six, seven times, once against Kudlap Singh here."

"That was long ago," said Jeremy.

"I'd like to see a rematch," Forbes said with a grin.

"In 1808, Thomas Jefferson refused a third term and retired forever from politics to Monticello," said Jeremy. "He knew when to move to new endeavors. Much like you and me."

"Whatever," Forbes said, rising and draping the towel around his neck. "Now, what do you want?"

I turned to Astaire and said, "Did you tell him?"

Astaire shook his head.

"A man named Willie Talbott was murdered today," I said. "Luna Martin worked for him as a dance instructor before—"

Mrs. Forbes had stopped her knee bends and was facing us with her hands on her hips.

"Go on," said Forbes, "Carlotta knows all about Luna. We're working it out. Just have a point when you get to the end."

I looked at Carlotta Forbes. Judging from the look she gave

her husband, if they were working it out, they had a lot of work left to do.

"Talbott had some information that might have helped us and the cops find her murderer," I said.

"Information?"

"Talbott was blackmailing her. I think it had something to do with one of Luna's clients when she was teaching at the On Your Toes ballroom. I went with Talbott to his apartment to get Luna's client list. Talbott tried to run with it. Someone put a hole in his chest and took the book."

"Sounds like a valuable book," Forbes said.

"You wouldn't have any idea where we might find it?" I asked.

Forbes suddenly did not look happy. "What are you sayin'?"

"I'm trying to find out who killed Luna Martin," I said. "That's what you said you wanted me to do."

Forbes strode toward me, throwing the towel in the general direction of the chair. When his nose was inches from mine, he whispered, "You want to watch us dance?"

"Sure," I said.

"You sit there and watch and in ten minutes you say, 'Good night, Mr. Forbes, Good night, Mrs. Forbes, Good night, Mr. Astaire,' and then you and your friend leave. You want to ask me questions, you call the hotel and leave a message and I'll get back to you. You understand?"

"Well—" I started, but Astaire was out of the corner and between us.

"Mr. Forbes and I have worked out a deal," Astaire said. "I give him and Mrs. Forbes five hours of lessons free of charge and my obligation to him is finished."

"What obligation?" I asked.

"Let's say it's in honor of the memory of Luna Martin," said Astaire.

"Arthur," Carlotta Forbes called. "Let's go. Who cares if some hoofer from the On Your Toes Dance Studio got tattooed with lead?"

"The glow of one warm thought is worth more to me than money," said Jeremy at my side.

"Jefferson?" I asked.

"Jefferson," Forbes said, moving away from me and across the room to his impatiently waiting wife.

"Toby, go," Astaire ordered. "I'll call you in the morning."

Astaire nodded to Kudlap Singh, who went to the phonograph and put on a scratchy version of a Horace Heidt fox-trot—at least I think it was a fox-trot.

I went to the chair Forbes had vacated and sat. Jeremy followed me, sat stiffly. Astaire walked to the waiting couple.

"Thomas Jefferson?" I whispered.

"A great president," Jeremy answered, his eyes fixed on the dancers before him.

"But why would a finger clipper from Detroit have a thing about Jefferson?"

"Thomas Jefferson was a brilliant statesman, inventor, businessman, and architect, admired by all. He also had an almost uncontrollable need for sex. A myriad of mistresses, including his own former slaves."

"You got a book about him I could read?" I said.

"Several," said Jeremy, and the couple were swirling around the floor.

Well, *swirling* is a little generous. Carlotta Forbes wasn't terrible. But Arthur was a disaster, worse than Luna had been. He stomped, slid, clomped, and trampled through the song while Astaire stood in the middle of the room, hand to his chin, watching and saying things like, "Slide, just brush the floor . . . shorter steps to the side . . . remember where you are in relation to the wall . . . good . . . left hand up. Elbows up. Smile. It's supposed to be fun."

After a long pause between records while Astaire quietly but animatedly huddled with the happy couple, he motioned for Singh to change the record. A Xavier Cugat rumba rattled through the room and the Forbeses tried to look like Volez and Yolanda and came out like Wheeler and Woolsey. When the song was mercifully over and Astaire had said—amazingly—"Good. We're getting somewhere," Forbes turned to me and Jeremy.

"You want a drink, Singh will get you one in the other room. Then I want you gone."

"A few more questions," I said. "How did you meet Luna Martin?"

"I said *out,*" Forbes said. "Singh, usher the visitors out of the house, now."

Singh dropped the needle on a fresh record and advanced on us accompanied by Guy Lombardo and the Royal Canadians.

Jeremy looked at me. I got up and said, "Did someone introduce you to Luna Martin?"

"Get them the hell out of here," Carlotta Forbes screamed.

The rest was fast. Singh reached for me. Jeremy grabbed his outstretched hand. Singh twisted away and threw an elbow at Jeremy's head. Jeremy sagged back over two of the blue chairs. I got out of the way fast. Singh stepped up on the blue chair and leaped at Jeremy, who had tumbled against the wall.

I looked at Forbes and his wife. They were smiling for the first time since we'd entered. Astaire stood, arms folded, watching with interest.

Jeremy and Singh were on the floor now. Jeremy threw Singh to one side and got him in a headlock. Singh broke loose, reversed, and got Jeremy in a full nelson. Jeremy's face and head were bright red and I thought of Alice Pallis Butler's warning to me about getting Jeremy in trouble. I moved in to help. Jeremy waved me away.

The two giants bounced around the room as the voice of Carmen Lombardo told us that love makes the world go 'round, Jeremy trying to break the hold, Singh holding tight. Flying past Carlotta Forbes, the two former wrestlers hit the mirror. It quivered but didn't break. Stunned, Singh released his prey. Jeremy gasped for air and then turned to face the massive Indian. They circled each other, breathing heavily, and then Jeremy lunged and the two men locked arms, head to head. They let out pained noises and Jeremy sank to one knee and then went over on his back, panting in defeat.

The record was over. It began to click as the needle repeated nothing.

Singh helped Jeremy up, grabbed my arm, and led both the staggering Jeremy and me to the door and into the hall past the Jefferson paintings. When we got to the front door, Singh let go of my arm, opened the door, and guided us out. We were greeted by the steady thumping of the derricks on the beach. Singh pushed the door closed behind us and said, "Once again I owe you, my friend."

Jeremy was no longer staggering or bent over in pain and defeat. He was upright, serious. Singh offered a hand. Jeremy took it.

"What the hell is this?"

"What you witnessed in there," Jeremy said, "was a slight variation on a routine Singh and I used on more than one occasion."

"Except for the chairs," said Singh. "I'm sorry about that."

"Added a touch," said Jeremy.

"I must go back," Singh said. "Be cautious, Peters. There are those who would like the matter to end here and who would do much to see that it happens."

The big Indian went back in the house.

"There was no possible victory in there, Toby," Jeremy said. "If I won, Kudlap Singh might lose his job, his income, the means of support for his considerable family. And he, like me, is not a young man. I had nothing to lose by losing."

"Could you have beaten him?" I asked, moving to the Buick.

"The danger comes in thinking about the battle in terms of winning and losing," he said, opening the car door. "You think of the battle as a contest, a test of your skills against those of another. Skills, power, and endurance, all cultivated and, perhaps most of all, an understanding of where you are and what you are in the universe at each moment."

"You've made it much clearer, Jeremy," I said, getting in the car.

"That was my intention," he said, sitting.

The front door of the house came open and Fred Astaire leaped from the steps and trotted down to the Buick. He leaned into Jeremy's open window and said, "Magnificent."

"Thank you," said Jeremy.

"That was some of the most inventive extemporaneous choreography I've ever seen," said Astaire with a smile, looking at me.

"Did Forbes or his wife know they were faking it?" I asked.

"No," said Astaire. "Their only regret was a lack of blood."

"We could have supplied that," said Jeremy.

"I'll bet you could," said Astaire. "Would you like to teach me some of that?"

"You wish to wrestle?" Jeremy asked.

"No, I wish possibly to develop a dance routine for my next movie based on a fight between two men. But I want it to look graceful and real. Amazing body control. I'd better get back in there and finish hour two. It strikes me that if someone is killing off the third-rate ballroom dancers in Los Angeles, Mr. and Mrs. Forbes could well be next on the list without my help. Oh, yes, I'll see what I can find out about your two questions, how did Forbes meet Luna and where did Luna live before she moved into the Monticello. I'll call you tomorrow."

Astaire danced back into the Forbeses' house and we pulled around his car and drove away.

We listened to "Can You Top This?" for about ten minutes. Peter Donald used his accents to tell a joke about an Irishman and an Italian trying to buy the same shirt. Then Senator Ford deadpanned a joke about a guy called Sandy who lost his shoes in the movie theater. He did all right on the laugh meter. Harry Hirschfield and Joe Laurie, Jr., told jokes that seemed pretty good to me but they didn't top the contestant's joke on the laugh meter.

I chuckled. Jeremy showed no emotion.

"It's funny, Jeremy," I said.

"Yes," he said. "Both of the Forbeses, husband and wife, are in great pain."

"They threw us out, threatened us with death and dismemberment, and you feel sorry for them?"

"I sense their pain," he said. "That is quite different from feeling sorry for them."

"Juanita said three would die," I said.

"I would not be surprised," said Jeremy.

And that was all we said till we parked in front of the Faraday Building.

"I wonder what time it is," I said, looking at my father's watch, which said it was four-twelve.

"I don't own a watch," said Jeremy, opening the door.

"I forgot," I said, getting out of Jeremy's car. "I'm tired and it's been a long day. Good night, Jeremy, and thanks."

Jeremy drove toward the corner where he made a right

and headed for his space behind the building. Three women, arm in arm and giggling, a little drunk, came down the street.

"Have the time?" I asked.

They stopped. They were all short of pretty, but makeup was doing a lot for them.

"Five after midnight," a pug-nosed blonde in the middle said.

"We're gonna turn into pumpkins," said a taller brunette, putting her hand over her mouth.

The other two girls thought this was hilarious. A sure ten on the laugh meter.

"Sherry's husband and our boyfriends just shipped out on the . . ." the blonde started but was cut off by Sherry, saying, "No names."

"That just slipped out and they just shipped out," the blonde said.

New laughter.

I left them on the street, looking for trouble or a cab. I couldn't tell if they'd gotten drunk to deal with their grief or were celebrating their liberty.

This part of Hoover was shut down by midnight. Stores were closed with no night-lights. Even Bowden's Bar across the street, which usually pushed the curfew, was asleep. I was pretty tired myself.

My car was at the corner where I'd left it, a parking ticket under the windshield wiper. This had been a bad day.

It suddenly got worse.

I opened the driver's-side door and leaned over to get in the Crosley, which is probably why the first bullet missed and went down the street. I ducked into the car and looked back over my shoulder, reaching for the glove compartment and my .38. The second shot whined off the roof of the car over my head.

There was no one on the street; no one I could see. The third shot shattered my rear window and thudded into the back of the passenger seat. I turned the key, ducked, and destroyed valuable tire rubber in a first-gear escape toward Main Street.

I checked the rearview mirror. Someone had stepped out of the Farraday shadows and was aiming a gun in my direction. I couldn't see who it was, but I did hear the next shot screech past me. I had my gun out of the glove compartment now, but I didn't know what I was going to do with it except sleep with it under my pillow.

Juanita had said something about my broken car window. She had also said something about three dancers dying and a fourth dancer . . .

The hell with it. I headed home.

Parking was tough after ten on Heliotrope, but my Crosley was small. I fit into a space between a fireplug and an old Ford. My .38 was in my hand and I checked the street to see if I had been followed. It looked safe. Of course, I couldn't be sure if someone had gotten here ahead of me and was hiding behind the bushes or leaning back into the shadows.

I checked the rear window. Shattered, glass all over the back seat. There was a scratch on the roof that went down to white metal. I couldn't tell how bad it was since the streetlights were cut for nightly curfew. Tomorrow.

I put my gun in my pocket but kept my hand on it. I can't shoot straight. The chances of my hitting a target more than ten feet away are small. But I could make a lot of noise if I had to.

Up the white wooden steps of Mrs. Plaut's boardinghouse. The door was locked. I took my key out quietly and went in. There was a dim light in the hall. Mrs. Plaut's door was closed. I started up the steps and heard something behind me, a door opening. I pulled out my gun, turned and sat on the step behind me.

"Mr. Peelers," said Mrs. Plaut with great exasperation. "That is a weapon in your hand."

She was wearing her oversized blue-flannel robe, which had belonged to the Mister when he had been alive and treading the byways of confusion with his lovely bride. She was also, thank God, wearing her hearing aid.

"I know, Mrs. Plaut."

"You meant to shoot Cornelia."

"Cornelia?"

"My bird. I am aware that you and your cat do not like Cornelia." Mrs. Plaut had a yellow budgie whose name changed with her depthless whims.

"I was not planning to shoot Cornelia, Mrs. Plaut. I promise you I will never harm Cornelia unless she attacks me in a rabid rage."

"If that should occur, you have my permission. You cannot, however, make the same promise for your cat."

"Dash isn't my cat. He just lives with me sometimes."

"He is, like all cats, stupid."

"Cats aren't stupid, Mrs. Plaut. They just don't like the rules."

She looked at the gun in my hand again. I stood up and put it in my pocket.

"I'm taking up a collection of guns," I said. "A hobby. To soothe my ragged nerves."

"A Police Positive Special Model—looks like a 1936—is hardly the weapon with which to begin a collection."

"You're right, Mrs. Plaut."

"I know where you can obtain an 1882 Adams and Tranter revolver for a reasonable price."

"You never fail to surprise me, Mrs. P.," I said.

"It is my lot in life."

"Someone tried to kill me tonight, Mrs. Plaut."

"That is not good," she said firmly. "Young men are dying all over the world in the war. People should not be trying to kill each other on the home front."

"Sounds reasonable to me," I said. "I've got to get some sleep."

I started back up the stairs.

"That is not likely," she said.

I grunted.

"Your sister is waiting in your room for you. She's been waiting for hours."

My hand went back to my gun.

I have no sister.

Chapter Ten

All Right Chillen, Let's Dance

A thin sheet of light shone under the door of my room and made a faint fan pattern on the wooden floor. I held the gun in my right hand, stood to the side of the door, and opened it quickly with my left as I jumped into the open doorway and leveled my weapon at a woman sitting on my sofa with a copy of *Woman's Day* in one hand, the other stroking Dash, who purred happily.

She looked up at me and smiled wearily.

I smiled back. She looked like she was about forty. Great teeth, blond hair pulled back, definitely clean and pretty. She wore a yellow dress that fit her snugly.

"Tough night?" she asked, looking at the gun in my hand.

She put down the magazine but continued to stroke the cat.

"Tough night," I said, closing my door, unable to place her familiar voice.

"I'm unarmed," she said.

"I can see that."

I put the gun back into my pocket. Guns are hell on pockets. I had a shoulder holster, one I bought when I was a cop in Glendale. I seldom used it and I almost never took the .38 from my closet.

"I have a message for you," she said now, stroking the contented Dash under his orange chin. "Violet would like you to bring the money you owe her in the morning."

"You're a friend of Violet?"

I was still standing. The only thing between us was the mattress, covered by a green blanket, on the floor.

"When I called your office, I talked to Violet. She gave me your address and asked me to remind you about the money. She said you lost a bet."

I moved to the table near the window, pulled out one of my two wooden chairs, and turned it toward her. I sat and tried to place that look and voice.

"You don't recognize me," she said.

I shrugged. "It's been a long day."

"Mr. Dutz, Music. How do we know radio announcers have small hands?"

"Because," I answered. "They say 'wee paws now for station identification.'" Dutz told that same dumb joke every semester. Clue number one, she had gone to Glendale High a long time ago. Dutz had been dead for almost twenty years.

"Don't have it yet?" she said, crossing her legs. They were good legs.

"You're not? . . ." I started.

"The flower was a purple orchid. You kissed me at my front door. You kept your mouth closed and your eyes open."

"Anita?"

"I clean up pretty good, Tobias," she said with a smile. "When you came to the diner the other day, I had put in twelve hours on my feet and had one hell of a Chinese headache. Not to mention that I wasn't wearing any makeup and I hadn't had my hair dyed and done in more than a month."

It was hard to believe this was the same tired woman who

had served me at Mack's diner and reminded me that I had taken her to the prom.

"Anita, what the . . . what are you doing here?"

She took Dash on her lap. Something the cat never allowed. Dash nuzzled against her breast. I was definitely waking up.

"You said you'd call. You didn't. I called. You didn't return my calls. I'm persistent. You want to hear a quick version of my life story since high school, the part I didn't cover at the diner?"

"I . . ."

"I think we should renew our acquaintance before we. . . . By the way, why don't you have a bed?"

"Bad back," I said. "Big guy gave me a bear hug right before the war. I was guarding Mickey Rooney. The big guy wanted to talk to him. I was in the way. Back's had a tendency to go out ever since. I sleep on my back on a hard mattress."

"See," she said. "We're getting to know each other. After Ozzie," she said, nuzzling her nose against Dash's, "I started college. One year at Scripps College for Women. Not easy when you're raising a kid. I put in odd hours at a diner on the Coast Highway. Got a part in a play we were putting on at Scripps with . . . you have coffee?"

"I'll make some," I said. "Keep talking."

She talked. I made coffee.

"Anyway, we put the play on with men from Pomona College. Men, boys. The play was *Mrs. Fowles's Mistake: A Comedy in Three Acts*. You know the kind of thing. Mistaken identities. Costumes. Women cheating on men who were cheating on women. I got bitten by the acting bug and a senior named Harold Sumner. We ran off, got married, found an apartment in Hollywood, and I tried to get into the movies. While I was ducking big-handed casting directors,

Harold was . . . dallying with a variety of ladies, young and not-so-young. Am I boring you?"

"No," I said, setting out two cups and saucers while the coffee perked on my hot plate.

"Bear with me," she said. "There's a point. I threw Harold out when I caught him with my mother. They were necking in the front seat of her car half a block from our apartment. My mother was a good-looking woman. Bad judge of men. It runs in the family."

"Want some toast with your coffee?" I asked.

She shrugged. I dropped two slices in the toaster and turned it on.

"Gave up on acting," she said. "Tried office work. Great Pacific Insurance. Businessmen and salesmen have hands just as big as casting directors. I married a nice older guy who owned a diner where I had lunch with a few other girls. Nice guy, Mack Chirikides. I went to work with him in the diner. Customers have big hands. Mack died. Found out he'd spent all his money on horses. There was mortgage to pay on the diner. A kid to raise. I kept working. You came in there the other day."

"Your kid?" I asked.

"One girl, with Ozzie," she said. "Lonny. She's married, lives in Sacramento. Husband's in the army. They've got one kid, Mal."

"You don't look like a grandmother," I said, gingerly pulling the toast out of the toaster and dropping it onto a plate.

"You?" she asked with a smile.

"Married Anne. Went to work for the Glendale Police force. Was asked to leave. Did security work for Warner Brothers. Got fired. Became a private detective. Lost Anne, wound up here."

The coffee was ready.

"Sugar and milk?" I asked.

"Black," she said. "I want to stay awake and I have to open the diner at seven."

She put Dash gently down on the sofa. He curled up and went to sleep.

"I fed him," she said, moving around the mattress and to the table. "Hope that's okay."

"Fine," I said, pouring the coffee into two mugs. I pulled some orange marmalade from the small refrigerator and put it on the table.

"Well," Anita said, taking a sip of coffee. "I've thought about you off and on over the years. You didn't have big hands and you didn't know how to kiss."

"That was a lot of years ago," I said. "I was a kid."

She nodded and said, "So was I. Since Mack died twelve years ago, I've been to bed with three men: a cop, a bread salesman, and a sergeant in the army. They all reminded me of you."

I didn't know what to say. I look in the mirror every morning to shave—well, almost every morning. What I see there is a definitely middle-aged man whose hair is rapidly going gray. I see a brown-eyed mug with a mashed-in nose. I do not see anyone close to Preston Stewart. I do not even see Humphrey Bogart.

"So," I said. "You tracked me down."

"To end the fantasy or bring it to life," she said.

"Nicely put," I said.

"I do a lot of reading."

She was looking at me over her cup. She held the cup in two hands. Her fingernails were short and very red. Her hands were rough. Her eyes were moist and perfect and when she put the cup down, her lips were red and full just like the girl I had kissed on prom night.

"Are you a little nuts?" I asked.

"Not usually," she said with a sigh. "I'm usually a patient counter cleaner who knows how to keep her customers happy and her bottom from being pinched. I don't think I've done a really wild thing in my life besides this. Are we going to keep talking?"

I got up and so did she. I moved to her. She pressed against me. The height was right. The feel of her breasts was right. I kissed her. Not like the kid at her door, like Gary Cooper. Long. Mouths open. She eased away and her hand went down between my legs. She smiled.

"Let's end the fantasy," I said.

"Let's see if we can find a new and better one," she answered.

Something woke me up. The first light of the sun was just glowing through the darkness. I blinked at the Beech-Nut clock on the wall. It was ten after six. I sat up. Anita came through the door.

"Wash room," she said. "I've got to get to the diner."

She leaned over and kissed me. I kissed back and tried to pull her gently back onto the mattress. She patted my hand and I let go.

"How's your fantasy?" I asked.

"Alive and well," she said with a smile.

"Movie Saturday?" I asked.

"Saturday night is busy," she answered. "You can have me all day Sunday."

I grinned and she left. I thought about Anne. I didn't much care at the moment if she married Preston Stewart or Tojo. If it weren't for the fact that someone had tried to kill me the night before, I would be in a damned good mood. My rear end didn't even hurt, though there was a tenderness to it that I had done my best to keep Anita from finding out about.

I threw the covers back and went through my ritual of standing up. First roll over on my hands and knees. Then put one foot on the floor and rise slowly. I waddled naked to the dresser in the corner, found a clean though holey pair of underpants and some socks that were not in need of serious mending, and put them on. Trousers were another problem. I went to the closet and found a pair of navy twills and a shirt with all the buttons. My poplin jacket was ruined, probably beyond repair after my fall on the roof where Willie Talbott was killed. I had a tan zipper jacket. The good news was that it was clean. The bad news was that the zipper didn't work. I pulled it out anyway.

Before I put on the shirt, I went down the hall to the communal bathroom. I thought I'd easily be the first one up. I was mistaken. Someone was taking a shower. I knocked on the door. Mr. Hill, the mailman who turned into an opera singer when he had some of Mrs. Plaut's Christmas grog in him, called, "Come in."

"It's me," I said loudly. "Toby Peters. Mind if I shave?"

"Shave," he called.

The room was steamy. That included the mirror. I shaved carefully with my Gem razor and a fresh blade. The day was going well so far. I managed to keep from cutting my throat or even nicking my chin.

"Early run," Mr. Hill said. "Why are you up? You're never up this early."

"Couldn't sleep," I said, gathering my shaving gear and trying to examine my face in the mirror, which had clouded again.

"Know how it is," he said. "Miss Reynal and I were up late in the parlor, talking."

Miss Reynal was the latest boarder, a redhead about forty-six, kind of pretty in a skinny way, which apparently was to Mr. Hill's liking.

"She's a fine woman," I said.

"Yes," said Mr. Hill in a rather throaty voice. Love was definitely in the air of the upstairs rooms of Mrs. Plaut's boardinghouse.

I dressed, put on my shoulder holster and gun, and covered them with my jacket that wouldn't zipper. Then Dash and I each had a big bowl of Wheaties and I was off on my quest for a killer.

Mrs. Plaut caught me as I tiptoed down the stairs. Mrs. Plaut seemed to sense when a boarder was going up or down.

"Mr. Peelers," she said, her hands folded over her broomstick frame. She was still or again wearing the Mister's robe.

"Yes, Mrs. Plaut."

"Your sister did not leave here till one hour past."

"We were up late talking about old times."

"What sane person would remain awake all night trying to remember old rhymes?" Mrs. Plaut was not wearing her hearing aid.

"She slept on the sofa," I shouted. Cornelia the budgie began chirping wildly.

"Your sister?"

"My sister."

"You do not look at all alike," she said suspiciously.

"You don't think so?" I shouted. "Strange, most people see the resemblance immediately. But I tend to think Anita looks like mom while I look like dad."

"Yes, you do seem to be quite mad. Here nor there. Sister or no sister. She stayed the night. Overnight guest rate is two dollars."

I got two dollars out of my wallet.

"New ration books Monday," she said, poking the two singles into the depths of the Mister's robe.

"I'll give you the food stamps, Mrs. Plaut."

"Dole's liniment," she said. "Takes care of your foot cramps like that." She snapped her fingers.

"Thank you," I shouted, trying to get past her.

"Wait," she said, holding up her hand.

I stood in the hall while she went back into her rooms. Cornelia was calming down but still pissed. Mrs. Plaut returned and handed me the world's largest muffin, or a small cake.

"Grandma Willitt's recipe for okra muffins," she said. "Tastes almost as good, but I used Crisco instead of butter. There's a war on."

"I know," I shouted, holding the muffin in two hands.

"Return the tinfoil," she said, pointing at the muffin.

I nodded and she went into her rooms, closing the door. I took a step toward the front door and Mrs. Plaut reappeared. She had a gun in her hand and it was aimed in the general direction of my crotch.

"Smith and Wesson thirty-eight Police Model Ten with a square butt. Neuter you in a flash."

I stood there with the okra muffin in my hand and smiled.

"Better weapon than that Police Special of yours," she said. "Belonged to the Mister."

"Like the robe," I shouted.

"Like everything in the house including the house," she said.

"I've got to get going."

"Give my hellos to your sister," Mrs. Plaut said, her weapon still aimed in my general direction. "I like her."

I retreated through the front door to the sunrise. No one shot at me. I headed for my car, wondering if I should drop the muffin and put my hand on my gun.

When I got to the Crosley, I knew something was wrong. The rear window was back, I went to the side of the car and looked in. The glass on the rear seat had been cleaned up.

Someone had even done a not-too-bad job of painting the bullet streak on the roof.

I got in the car. There was an envelope on the passenger-side seat. My name was on the envelope. I opened it. There were five crisp hundred-dollar bills in it and a handwritten note:

> Peters. I clean up after myself. Take the money and forget the investigation. I don't want to clean up blood. Last night was a warning. There will be no more.

There was no signature. I put the note back in the envelope and looked at the bills. I folded them, shoved them in my pocket, and drove back to the Farraday Building.

My hope, as it had been at Mrs. Plaut's, was that it was still too early for any of the tenants to be in, though I knew Jeremy would be up and about with his soapy bucket and patient determination, ready for combat with grime.

I parked in front. There were plenty of spaces and I didn't expect to be there very long.

The door of the Farraday was locked. I figured it was no later than seven or seven-fifteen. I used my key and went in. The dim lights were still on and the Farraday was silent. I went up the stairway slowly, trying to make sense out of what was going on. I had no success. I did have five hundred dollars and a note. Everybody was giving me money—Astaire, Forbes, the guy who shot at me. I was rapidly gaining some sense of financial security. My love life had shown a definite and surprising improvement. And I had no idea who killed Luna Martin or Willie Talbott.

There were no lights on in the offices of Minck and Peters, but the door was open. Could be lots of reasons. Shelly or Violet had forgotten to lock it last night. Someone was inside waiting to kill me. Or, most unpleasant to contemplate,

Shelly had arrived painfully early. When I opened the inner door I found that the worst had come to pass.

Shelly was in his dental chair. Violet was leaning over him, their faces close together. The lights were out and the venetian blinds were closed, letting in hints of sunlight.

"Good morning," I said.

Violet jumped away from Shelly and Shelly blinked twice at me and shifted in his chair. He didn't have his white smock on yet. All he was wearing were his trousers, a shirt, and a dazed look.

"Toby?" he asked.

"Put your glasses on, Shel," I said.

Shelly groped in his pocket and came up with his thick, heavily fingerprinted glasses. He perched them on the end of his nose. "Toby," he repeated, only not as a question.

"Dr. Minck has had a tragedy," said Violet, who was wearing a tight-fitting dress that matched her name.

"Mildred threw me out," Shelly cried.

"And Dr. Minck called and asked me to come in early to give him some support," explained Violet, checking her hair for strays.

"It's not what it looks like, Toby," Shelly said.

"I know," I said. "If you touched Violet, and I can't imagine her letting you, her husband would be through that door when the war was over to batter your misshapen body with his lethal fists. Am I right, Violet?"

"One hundred percent, Mr. Peters, but Dr. Minck has been a gentleman."

"A despondent gentleman," Shelly said, putting his head in his pudgy-fingered hands. "A depressed gentleman. A gentleman on the verge of breakdown. A gentleman . . ."

"How many times has Mildred thrown you out, Sheldon?" I asked.

He shrugged and threw up his hands.

"Five? Ten? More?"

"This one is different, Toby. She accused me of . . . you know, with Mrs. Gonsenelli. She just saw her picture and . . ."

"Saw her picture?" I asked.

"In my wallet," Shelly explained.

"You carry Violet's photograph in your wallet?"

"Behind my driver's license. How was I to know Mildred would go through every card in my wallet?" he said, almost weeping.

"Can I get you coffee?" Violet volunteered.

"Black for Dr. Minck, cream and sugar for me."

I reached into my pocket for change but Violet waved me off, saying, "You can pay me when I get back and you pay up for the fight."

"Mauriello wasn't trying," I said.

"He lost," Violet said reasonably, moving toward the door. "You'll be all right, Dr. Minck?"

Shelly was choked with emotion. He couldn't speak through his tears. He waved her on and she went out the door.

"Shel," I said. "You can stop. She's gone."

Shelly looked over the top of his glasses, saw that I was telling the truth, and said angrily, "Five more minutes, Toby. Five more and she would have felt so sorry for me that . . ."

"I don't think so, Shel. Did Mildred really throw you out?"

"Yep," he said, getting out of the chair. "But she'll get over it. Always does. Toby, I love that woman."

"Which one?"

"My wife." Shelly searched the floor for his shoes, found them, and picked them up.

"I'm checking my messages and then I'm out of here."

"I think maybe the police believed me," Shelly said, grunting into his shoes as he sat in his dental chair. "A captain named Cawelti came by the house last night. One of the reasons besides Violet that Mildred threw me out. Wanted to know why Luna Martin pointed at me before she fell down dead. Told him I didn't know. Asked a lot of questions about you."

"We're old ballet-school classmates," I said.

"You went to ballet school?" Shelly had paused in putting on his shoes and looked at me as if I had surprised him with a secret identity.

"Sure, before I became a cop. Starred in *Swan Lake*," I said.

"No," he said.

"No," I agreed.

"Fingers," he said. "He's not trying to kill me, cut off my fingers?"

"No."

"Can I believe you? I mean, really believe you?"

"Have I ever lied to you, Sheldon?"

"Many times," Shelly said, looking around the office for his smock. "Wait, maybe Luna Martin wasn't pointing at me before she died. Maybe she was pointing at someone behind me. After all, she was dying."

"There wasn't anyone behind you," I reminded him.

An idea struck me. There had been no one behind Shelly but there was . . . something. Then the idea seemed stupid.

The outer door opened and Violet called, "Someone open the door. My hands are full."

I moved to the door and opened it. Violet came in with two paper cartons of coffee.

"When you finish the coffee," she said, handing me one, "rinse it and put it in the wastepaper bin in your office."

"I have a wastepaper bin in my office?"

"War effort," she said seriously. "Dr. Minck said it was okay."

I looked at Shelly. He was, with Violet's return, once again on the verge of suicide. Violet handed him the other carton of coffee. He took it and touched her hand, saying, "God bless you, Violet. I don't know how I would have gotten through the morning without you."

Violet smiled, patted his hand, and turned to face me. "Calls," she said, looking up at the ceiling and biting her charming lower lip. "A Mr. Astor, said you had his number. And a Mr. Forbes. Forbes left a number. I put it on your desk. He said he had to see you first thing this morning. Said it was very important. And a Mr. Canton called. Said you owe him money and would you please pay. Only he didn't say 'please.'"

"That it?" I asked, moving to my office and trying not to spill coffee.

"That's it," she said, following.

"Don't leave me," Shelly called.

"Be right back," Violet said.

Shelly was sobbing now and looking around the dental office as if he had never seen it before. "Oh Death," he wept. "Where is thy sting."

I went into my office. Violet followed me and closed the door. In the corner was a cardboard box already half full of newspapers and old dental magazines.

"Don't worry, Mr. Peters," she said. "Dr. Minck is a cuddly puppy dog. And I know a fake cry when I hear one. He won't touch me."

"Good," I said, moving behind my desk and looking down at the message from Forbes.

"You've got a glow, Mr. Peters," she said.

"A glow?"

"Like you've . . . I mean like . . . You have a date last night?"

"Yes."

She shook her head knowingly. I reached into my pocket.

"Good coffee," I said. "How much do I owe you?"

"Twelve dollars," she said.

I handed her one of the five one-hundred-dollar bills that had been in the envelope.

"I don't have change for this."

"I don't want change. I want you to go out and find another job. I'll give you some leads if you want them."

"I can take care of myself," she said. Violet had married Angelo "Rocky" Gonsenelli, middleweight contender, four days before he shipped out. She had taken care of herself till now and it was none of my business. "You don't want change?"

"No," I said.

"You're not fishing for . . ."

"No," I said.

"Good," she said happily. "You don't know how much I need this. Thanks. Remember to drop the cup in the wastepaper bin when you're finished."

And she was gone.

I drank my coffee, looked out the window, tossed the cup in the general direction of the box in the corner, missed, retrieved the cup, and dropped it on top of yesterday's *L.A. Times*. Then I called the number Forbes had left.

"Yes?" a man's voice answered after the fourth ring.

"Forbes?"

"What?"

"Peters."

"Peters. Get to the hotel. Room 813. Now. I've got something I want you to bring to the cops. It'll mean a bonus for you."

He hung up. I looked up at the Dali painting that covered

one wall. The two babes were still content, in their beaming mother's arms.

I looked at the wall in front of me. Phil and I still stood next to my father in the photograph, and our dog Kaiser Wilhelm looked directly at the camera. I suddenly wondered who had taken that photograph. I pulled out my notebook and wrote the question for Phil on a fresh sheet.

I called Fred Astaire. A woman answered after five rings. I gave her my name and about twenty seconds later Astaire was on the phone.

"I think I've got that problem taken care of, as I told you last night," he said.

"Maybe," I said, "but Luna Martin and Willie Talbott are still dead. Someone took a shot at me last night and left a note on my front seat telling me to stop looking for Luna's killer."

"That wasn't the problem I was referring to," said Astaire. "But it certainly tops mine."

I told him about the call from Forbes and he said he'd meet me at the Monticello.

"I don't think you should go," I said. "But what I think doesn't matter, does it?"

"It matters," Astaire said, "but it doesn't determine. Look, I've got a day before the fund raiser and then I have to go on that bond tour. I'd like something settled here before I go. See you at the hotel."

He hung up and so did I.

In the dental office, Shelly was now wearing his smock and shoes. The cigar had not yet appeared. Violet was holding his coffee cup and Shelly was back in the chair still sobbing. Violet and I exchanged looks and I was gone.

Chapter Eleven

Do Come A-Waltzing Matilda

Cotton Wright was on duty at the Monticello Hotel parking lot. I pulled in, got out, and handed him the keys to the Crosley. He tried to place me and scratched at the metal plate in his head.

"Your head humming?" I asked.

"Lots and loud. You a veteran?"

"Yes," I lied.

Cotton beamed and pursed his lips, plunging his hands into the pockets of his overalls. "I could tell," he said. "I'll park you someplace special. You know I'm a veteran?"

"I know," I said. "You told me."

"I did?"

"Not today."

"The Maginot Line is gone," Cotton confided, looking around to be sure no one was listening.

"I've heard," I whispered back. "You know Mr. Forbes?"

Cotton held up his right hand and mowed down the fingers one by one. "Always gives me half a dollar," he said.

"He come here last night?"

"Wasn't on duty overnight," said Cotton. "That was Moe Schroeder, definitely a veteran. Mr. Forbes's car was here when I got here though. Six o'clock in the A.M."

"See you in a while," I said, turning toward the hotel.

"Mr. Forbes is not a veteran," he called after me.

I stored this valuable information and walked the half block to the entrance of the Monticello. The place was just coming alive. A handful of people were heading out for breakfast and another handful were gabbing and dozing in the lobby. They looked like they were waiting for a tour bus.

The fey desk clerk I had talked to the day before was behind the desk, dealing with a guest who complained with both hands. She was frantic about something and the clerk was responding with perfect calm. He saw me cross to the elevator and gave me a nod.

I was alone in the elevator. I checked my .38 and put it loosely in the holster. God protect anyone in the room, including me, if I had to use it. The elevator eased to eight and I got out. It all looked familiar. Room 813 was the last one down the corridor. I knocked and waited. Nothing. I knocked again and the door opened.

Fred Astaire was standing in the doorway. He was dressed completely in black—trousers, shirt, with a red tie and no jacket. He looked both ways down the corridor and pulled me into the room, closing the door behind me.

"Look at this," he said.

I looked around the room. Standard hotel-suite living room. Big, lots of light-colored old French-looking furniture, a great view. The same room I'd been in before. On the coffee table in front of a Louis-the-something sofa sat the wire recorder Willie Talbott's and Luna Martin's call had been recorded on. Someone had beat the hell out of the machine. My guess was the job had been done by a baseball bat or a sledgehammer.

"I see," I said.

"No, you don't," Astaire said, motioning me to follow him to the open door to the left.

We stood in the doorway. The window drapes were up and the morning sun spread like a blanket over the late Arthur Forbes. He was naked and on his back. His eyes were open and seemed to be fascinated by something on the ceiling. I looked up. There was nothing there. I looked back at Forbes's body. His chest was a wet, dark-red pool. The handle of a knife stuck out of his belly. Forbes's hands were clasped around the handle.

"Suicide?" Astaire asked.

"Multiple wounds," I said. "You don't commit suicide by stabbing yourself six or seven times. It looks like he was trying to get the knife out when he died. I'd say you don't have to give any more dance lessons to Arthur Forbes."

I motioned to Astaire to stay at the doorway and went to the side of the bed, being careful not to touch anything. I checked Forbes's fingers. They were all there.

"What happened?" I asked.

Astaire shrugged and said, "I came. I knocked. The door was open a crack. I stepped in, saw the wire recorder, and then found . . . him. You knocked a minute or two later."

"You touch anything?"

Astaire closed his eyes and tried to think. "Doorknobs, bedpost."

"Good," I said, wiping both bedposts with the end of the bedspread. "I think you should quietly get out of here and forget you came."

"Someone may have seen me," he said. "I think the desk clerk recognized me."

"I'm sure the desk clerk recognized you," I said, looking around for a clue and seeing none. "We lock the door behind us and say we knocked and got no answer."

"Can't do that, Toby," Astaire said.

"You don't tell lies?" I said, moving past him into the living room and trying to remember if I had touched anything but the wreckage of the wire recorder.

"Not illegal ones," he said.

"How was Forbes as a dancer?" I asked, looking at Astaire.

"Terrible, why?"

"Three bad dancers are dead," I said.

"You think someone is killing people who can't do the fox-trot?"

"No," I said. "Look, you don't have to lie. But you don't have to be here when the police come. We go somewhere. I call the police, tell them where to find Forbes, and you go home or wherever you were going. If the police come to talk to you, tell them we reported the murder and on my advice you went home. You buy that?"

"I'm thinking," Astaire said.

"Think on the way downstairs," I said and went to the front door.

"I don't have to think about it," said Astaire with a sigh. "I'm calling the police from the lobby and waiting for them."

"Suit yourself," I said with a shrug and opened the door to the hallway.

Captain John Cawelti was standing there, his hand up to knock. Behind him was Steve Seidman.

"Captain, we were on the way down to call you," I said. "Forbes is in the other room, dead."

"I know," said Cawelti, touching his center-parted red hair to be sure it hadn't all fallen out.

He moved past us with Seidman behind him. I mouthed, "Where's Phil?" Seidman shook his head.

"Your brother is on special assignment," Cawelti said, looking down at the remnants of the wire recorder. "I wanted this one. Got a call that Arthur Forbes had been murdered and that none other than Mr. Fred Astaire had done him in."

Cawelti turned suddenly and faced Astaire, who gave the red-faced captain a patient smile.

"Big name? Big publicity?" I asked.

"Me?" said Cawelti. "Would I care about that kind of thing?" He moved to the bedroom and stood for a beat before going in. Steve Seidman stayed with us and whispered, "Cawelti assigned Phil to host a group of small-town mayors wanting a tour and rundown on the L.A. Police Department and its operations."

It was the very thing Phil hated most and Cawelti knew it.

"Mr. Forbes, him dead," said Cawelti, emerging from the bedroom with a smile. "Seidman, call the M.E., investigation unit, fingerprints, the usual. And don't use the phones in here."

"Right, Captain," Seidman said, moving to the door and out.

Cawelti was happy. He motioned for us to sit in two of the living-room chairs while he took another. He should have taken us out of the room instead of sitting us down on potential evidence.

"You want to know what the caller told me?" Cawelti asked.

"Man or woman?" I asked.

"I'm in a good mood, Peters, so I'll tell you. Man, high voice and a handkerchief or something over the phone. Caller said none other than Mr. Fred Astaire himself had murdered the prominent Mr. Arthur Forbes. Story I got was Forbes insisted that Astaire give him and his wife dance lessons and Astaire said he'd rather see them both dead. Astaire came here to have it out with Forbes. Forbes is dead."

"Caller knew a hell of a lot," I said.

"You let me worry about that, Peters. How about you tell me how you helped Astaire here kill Forbes and probably kill Luna Martin and Willie Talbott?"

"We got here a few seconds before you," I said. "You can ask the desk clerk. We found the body and were on the way downstairs to call you."

"That your best story?" Cawelti asked, looking at both of us as he sat comfortably with his hands folded and legs crossed.

"That," said Astaire, "is the truth."

"I can see you on the bottom of the *Times* front page," Cawelti said, looking at Astaire. "You know the look they catch you with, your mouth open, eyes wide from the flash."

"John," I said.

"Captain," he corrected.

"Captain," I amended. "You and I have a long history. We don't have to make Mr. Astaire a part of it."

"I'm afraid we do," Cawelti said with a sigh of false sympathy and a shake of his head.

"Look . . ." I began but never got the new ploy on the table because Seidman was back.

"That was fast," Cawelti said, looking up at him.

"Floor maid was cleaning a room," Seidman said. "Flashed the badge and told her I needed the phone. Commissioner says no publicity, none on Astaire till we know for sure with a certainty he's involved. Commissioner emphasized 'no publicity' and 'with a certainty.'"

"You called the commissioner?" Cawelti said in disbelief.

"Yes," said Seidman, "and the M.E. and everyone else."

"You had no goddamn right to call the commissioner," Cawelti said, pushing himself out of the chair. His face was crimson again.

"Figured he might want to know," said Seidman evenly. "He seemed to appreciate it."

"You," Cawelti said, pointing a finger at Seidman, "are going to apply for a transfer from the Wilshire."

"Already did. When you were promoted. And if I don't get the transfer, I've got an offer from the Glendale Police. Good offer. War's made a lot of departments shorthanded." It was more than I had heard Steve Seidman say in the fifteen or so years I had known him.

"Get the hell out of here," Cawelti shouted, losing the last of his cheerful mood.

Seidman looked at me and Astaire and moved out of the suite slowly, closing the door behind him.

"If you were to ask me . . ." Astaire began.

"I'll ask you plenty," Cawelti said, turning on him. "But I'll decide what to ask. Nobody is going to step on me, nobody. Not you, not the commissioner, not Louis Goddamn B. Mayer. I tore my way up. I did my job. I've got no friends. No family. Nothing but this job and my pride and I'm not going to lose them and I'm not going to let anybody, *anybody,* step on me. You get it?"

"Got it," Astaire said, holding up his hands to indicate that he was backing off from verbal battle.

"Peters?" Cawelti said, turning on me.

I didn't even answer.

"I know a bartender, a clerk at Ralph's grocery," Cawelti went on, having lost what little reserve of patience he had held back. "I've got a cat and that's it. What I've got, I fought for. I deserve."

"No one is arguing with you, John," I said. "Captain."

"Come on," said Cawelti, motioning for us to get up.

We got up.

"We'll have a nice talk in my office and wait for some results."

"I really have to . . ." Astaire began, looking at his watch.

"I'm getting calm," Cawelti said, his voice dropping. "Do I look calm?"

"You're getting there," Astaire said.

"My old man died at the age of fifty," Cawelti said. "Stroke. I'm calm. I don't care what you have to or where you have to do anything. We are going to my office."

And we went.

We had coffee in Cawelti's office. When Phil was in here it was bare walls, table, and a couple of chairs, a monk's cell. Cawelti had decorated. Citations covered one wall, along with photographs of John Cawelti shaking hands with mayors and movie people, including Joe E. Brown, Merle Oberon, Tyrone Power, and the Ritz Brothers. Every cop had photographs like this. Few of them put them on their office walls.

On the wall opposite the desk was an aerial map of the city and a big framed photograph of a man who looked suspiciously like John Cawelti.

"My father," Cawelti said when he caught Astaire looking at the photograph. "Taught me everything I know. Made it to lieutenant before he died. Hated the sadistic son of a bitch, but he taught me."

Cawelti drank some coffee. So did Astaire and I as we sat across from him.

We had been through the basics. Forbes's call to me. My call to Astaire. I even told him about the shots that had been taken at me and I showed him the note I'd found in my front seat. "Anyone can write a note," he said, hardly glancing at it and throwing it back at me in a ball.

"Not if they're illiterate," I said, pocketing the note.

"How's this fit for a case?" Cawelti said. "Luna Martin was making demands on your client here. He hired you. You got rid of Luna Martin. Willie Talbott had some evidence about

Astaire and Luna Martin. You got rid of Talbott. Then Forbes found out, told you to come over, said he was going to pickle a few of your digits, and you got rid of him. The two of you have been present at three murders in the last three days. I call that more than a coincidence."

"And less than evidence," I said.

"We didn't kill anyone," Astaire said. "This is crazy. If you'd just let me explain . . ."

Cawelti took a hurried sip from his coffee, put it down, and held up a hand to stop Astaire.

The phone rang. Cawelti picked it up and said, "Captain Cawelti . . . yes . . . yes . . . and that's the best you can do? Thanks."

He hung up and looked at us.

"Arthur Forbes was stabbed seven times in the chest and abdomen, probably with the knife he was holding onto. Can't tell the exact time of death, but about the time you were both in that room. So, what have I got? Luna Martin had her throat cut. And Willie Talbott was shot with a thirty-eight. You own a thirty-eight, Peters."

I reached under my jacket, took out my gun, and handed it to him. "They won't match," I said.

"And finally," Cawelti said, laying the gun on the desk in front of him, "Arthur Forbes, alias Fingers Intaglia, takes a knife to the heart. Knife has no fingerprints. Anything either one of you have to say?"

"We want to call a lawyer," I said.

"Leib?" asked Cawelti.

"Leib," I confirmed.

"That . . ." Cawelti began.

"Careful, John," I said. "I plan to tell him everything you've said."

Cawelti got up, drained the last of his coffee, and dropped the empty cup in the wastebasket next to his desk.

"You wait here," he said, pointing to the floor, and off he went.

"You think . . ." Astaire began when the door had closed, but I cut him short with a finger to my lips.

I grabbed the pad on Cawelti's desk, turned it around, and with the pencil I took out of my pocket wrote, "Ten to one he's listening to us."

Astaire nodded and I crumpled the note and threw it in the wastebasket.

"Good coffee," I said.

"Very good."

"Probably A & P Eight O'Clock."

"Good coffee," Astaire said again. "Captain Cawelti seems like a decent guy."

"Decent? He's the best. I've heard he volunteers down at the Mission Street Soup Kitchen on his days off."

"Really?" asked Astaire. "He really think we killed Forbes?"

"Strangled Luna, shot Talbott, and stabbed Forbes," I answered. "Multitalented."

"Versatile," said Astaire. "Ever try to plant avocados?"

"Can't say I have. But I've got an aspidistra flying in a window box."

The door burst open. Cawelti stood there.

"I've been decent to you," he said.

"John, we've just been saying nice things about you," I said.

"Make your call to Leib," Cawelti said. "I'm holding you both on suspicion of murder."

And he was gone again.

"I've got a very good lawyer," Astaire said as I reached for the phone.

"We don't want a good lawyer," I said. "We want Marty Leib."

Marty wasn't in his office. His secretary, Charlene, gave me a number where he could be reached when I told her it was an emergency. I looked at the door, expecting Cawelti to return. He didn't. I found Martin Raymond Leib at the offices of the Clarkborough Advertising Agency.

"How important?" Marty asked.

I told him. And I told him fast. Marty has been known to charge by the minute.

"Not bad," he said. "Cash up front."

"Cash up front," I repeated.

Astaire nodded.

"You say nothing more to the police without me present," Marty said. "Nothing. Not a word. Don't even cough and above all don't fart."

"Not a fart. Not a word. Not a sneeze."

"You've got the idea," Marty said and hung up.

One hour and twenty minutes later Astaire and I were in Martin Leib's Cadillac, heading back to the Monticello for Astaire's car and my Crosley.

Marty had taken a check from Astaire and pocketed it. He was breathing fast and heavy. "Desk clerk at the Monticello confirms that Forbes called you, Toby," Marty said, adjusting his tie in a useless attempt to get comfortable. "Even by chance heard a few words of the conversation."

"Lucky for us," I said.

"Well," said Marty, "I doubt if they've got nearly enough to get a bill on any of the murders on either of you. I'll call the commissioner and get him to keep sitting on this."

"You know the commissioner?" Astaire asked.

Astaire and I were in the back seat. Marty's neck was too thick and his body too heavy to face us when he answered, "Well indeed, but Rusty and I don't roll in the same circles. We occasionally deal, though. I'm known as one of the best if not the best shyster in the business. Call to the commissioner is free if I get a personally autographed photo."

"Consider it done, Mr. Leib," said Astaire.

"You're a fan, Marty?" I asked.

"I was bitten or at least kicked in the can by Terpsicore when I was a child. Wife and I are good enough to compete in the ballroom regionals and we've got a couple of ribbons."

I couldn't imagine all three hundred and fifty pounds of Marty Leib waltzing around a dance floor.

"Weren't for you," Marty said, looking at Astaire in his rearview mirror, "Toby would be back in the Wilshire lockup playing 'Camptown Races' on a toilet-paper kazoo. I had to walk out on a cash-paying client facing a major fraud charge."

"Why don't I give your client an autographed photo too?" asked Astaire.

"Harley is not a dance fan," said Marty, pulling into the parking lot at the Monticello. "I'm sure he would be close to ecstasy and agreeing to any terms I might have for conducting his defense were he to be given an autographed photo of Rita Hayworth."

"Man has good taste," said Astaire. "I'm sure I can manage that."

Astaire and I got out of the car and Marty rolled down the window to say, "Mr. Peters has my office address. It's Leib. L-e-i-b not L-i-e-b. And 'Marty' not 'Martin.'"

"Got it," said Astaire.

Marty drove off with a wave.

"I've got to get to a rehearsal," Astaire said, looking at his watch. "Then I've got to explain all this to my wife. What are you going to do?"

"Locate my car, grab a sinker and coffee at a diner, and find a killer," I said. "I'm a veteran," I told Cotton Wright as he slouched toward us. "So is my friend."

Cotton saluted, took our stubs, and went in search of our autos.

"Careful, Toby," Astaire said, touching my arm.

"Do my best," I answered.

He got in his car and drove away. Cotton brought the Crosley.

"Someone shrunk your car," he said, easing his way out from behind the steering wheel.

"Rain, maybe," I said, giving him a half dollar and climbing in.

"Rain doesn't shrink metal," he said. "If it did, I'd be one of those pinheads in the circus."

It made sense to me.

Ten minutes later I was at Mack's Diner at the crowded counter exchanging smiles with Anita, who brought me a tuna on toast and a coffee.

"Trust me with this," she whispered, placing the sandwich in front of me.

"I'll trust you with a lot more," I said. She patted my hand and went off to a calling customer.

The Negro guy sitting next to me drinking a bowl of vegetable soup piled high with Saltines examined my sandwich without turning his head. Twenty minutes and two coffees later the lunch crowd was thinning out, the Negro had gone, and Anita came over to sit. She wore little makeup and her uniform was a size loose. She caught me looking and said, "Keeps the big hands away."

"I remember," I said.

"Came to say the fantasy's over?" she asked.

"Came to say we should try making it real."

"Sounds good to me," Anita said, pushing a stray curl back behind her ear. She cast a glance around the diner to check that no one was looking at us and gave me a quick kiss on the lips. She tasted like coffee. "You've got my number?" she asked.

"On a napkin near my heart," I answered.

"You know, this might be fun."

"Already is," I said.

I dropped a dollar on the counter and stopped at the pay phone just outside. I had a stack of nickels and used most of them to reach the number I wanted. When she answered and said hello, I hung up.

I had a long day of driving ahead of me.

Chapter Twelve

I'm Gonna Dance Out Both My Shoes

The Mozambique looked like it was designed by an alcoholic art director who had worked one too many B pictures with Jon Hall. The green walls were covered with bad paintings of jungle animals and trees but it was hard to see them. The lights were always down and dim at the Mozambique, to give it atmosphere and to cut down on the cleanup. The bar was long and dark wood. There were half-a-dozen tables and four red-leatherette booths. Beyond the tables was a platform on which Lou Canton sat at a piano, playing "After You've Gone" for a weeping woman who was nursing a drink at one of the tables.

"Wow," screamed Sidney, the ancient cockatoo, when I moved to the bar.

"Wow to you, Sid," I said, sitting on a stool.

Lester Gannett, owner and bartender, rushed over to me. "Pevsner—"

"Peters," I corrected.

"I don't care what your name is now. Just get the hell out, okay? Last time you were in here my tenor was murdered and I had five hundred dollars' damage from a riot you started. Time before that, when you were still a cop, your partner jumps on the stomach of a customer."

Lester's complexion was bad. He needed some sunlight and decent food.

"I think you're getting scurvy, Lester," I said.

"I'm not gettin' scurvy. I'm gettin' scared. Pev . . . Peters. Come on."

"Gotta talk to Lou," I said. "I owe him money."

"Give it to me. I'll give it to him. I gotta tell you the truth here. You make me nervous."

"How's Jeannie?" I asked. Jeannie was Lester's teenage daughter. Last time I had been in the Mozambique, Jeannie had been picking up sailors and getting them to buy drinks from dad.

"Fine," Lester said with a sigh. "She's startin' college up in San Francisco. Okay. One drink. One drink. On me. You take care of your business with Lou and you get out. Pepsi, right?"

"You got it, Lester. How's Lillian?" Lillian was Lester's wife. Before the war Lillian had played the customers at the bar. But time had caught up with her and the iced tea in the highball glass had been turned over to Jeannie.

"Lillian," Lester sighed, pouring me a Pepsi. He nodded at the woman at the table listening to Lou.

"Lillian?" I asked, turning to get a better look at the woman.

Lester nodded again. Time had passed Lillian Gannett and left her standing in its tire tracks.

I picked up my drink and started toward the little bandstand.

"Peters, come on. Do me a favor. The before-dinner trade starts coming in in a few minutes."

I ignored him and moved to the table where Lillian Gannett was looking deep into her drink. It was dark and had a cube in it but I was sure it wasn't iced tea.

Lou looked at me and launched into a downbeat version of "We're in the Money."

Lillian looked even worse up close. Her hair was going white at the roots and needed brushing. The pores on her cheeks were uncovered by powder and were large, probably from too much barroom darkness and too many packs of Camels. She looked up at me.

"Got the wrong girl, soldier," she said. Her eyes were the greenest I had ever seen. She still had that.

"Got the right woman, Lil," I said.

She did her best to focus on my face. "The nose," she said. "You were a cop."

"Pevsner. Tobias Pevsner," I reminded her.

She looked toward her husband at the bar. Lester was setting up a pair for a couple of old guys in overalls who had just come in.

"Lester would rather not see you," she said.

"I finish my Pepsi, give Lou some money I owe him and I'm out of here."

Lou was humming along with the piano now. He was playing something I didn't recognize.

"Don't correct me if I'm wrong, but didn't I pick you up one night, back in . . . maybe '30? You were gonna get married. Lester was busy. We went to . . ."

"It was my partner who was getting married. I didn't get married till a few years later."

"But you and I did . . ."

"Yeah," I said. "We did, Lil."

"You could be Jeannie's father," she said, looking at me as well as she could.

"No," I said. "Jeannie was already nine or ten."

Lillian pursed her lips, shrugged, and took another drink. "To fading memories," she said.

"To fading memories," I said, finishing my Pepsi and nodding to Lou.

"Ladies and gentlemen," Lou said, standing at the piano and touching his thin, dyed mustache to be sure it was still there, "there'll be a short break. When I return, I'll be taking requests. And remember, at eight tonight, the world-renown chanteuse Miss Evelyn will be on this very stage to sing her greatest hits."

Lou wandered back through the curtains and disappeared. No one applauded. Lillian did not even look up.

"I'll see you around, Lillian," I said, touching her shoulder.

"Any afternoon, same place," she said. "Jeannie's going to college."

"I know," I said.

"Lester's trying to get my niece Holly to work the bar. Her husband's on the night shift at Lockheed."

"Good luck," I said.

I took the short step up to the stage and followed Lou through the curtains. There was a door beyond. I opened it and made my way to Lou's dressing room and home. He was sitting in front of the mirror adjusting his hair. He looked up at me.

"It's a living," he said, his eyes looking in the general direction of the stage he had just left.

I took out my wallet and handed him two twenties and four singles.

"Generous," he said.

"Fred Astaire's paying. That cover taxis and fixing the piano at the Monticello?"

"Covers it and more," Lou said, pocketing the money.

"Then I'll ask more," I said, sitting on the edge of Lou's bed.

He had to turn to face me. "Ask," he said.

"When Luna Martin was killed, you were out in the hallway in front of the ballroom. Did you see her?"

"In the hall?"

"Yeah."

"I don't think so," Lou said, biting his lower lip and trying to remember. "Ask me who played second cornet for Sam-Sam Anderson and the Hoochie Koochies in '08 and I'll tell you. But yesterday . . ."

"Give it a try, Lou."

"Someone went past me. A woman in white. I was thinking piano. I think there was someone with her. I think they were talking."

"Arguing?"

"Arguing," he said. "Maybe. I had other things on my mind."

"You didn't look at the guy?"

"Who remembers?"

"Thanks, Lou," I said, getting up. "If you remember anything . . ."

"It'll be a miracle. But I do remember you said something about wanting me to meet a certain lady of age and means."

"Mrs. Plaut," I said.

"That, I remember," Lou said.

There was a knock at Lou's door and then it opened before he could say, "Come in."

A woman, her dark hair pulled back, her lips full and very dark, stuck her head in. "No sink in my dressing room," she said, ignoring me.

"Take it up with the management, Evelyn."

"Management says to take it up with you."

"All right," Lou said. "I'll build you a sink. I'll build you a bath with marble. Just give me a couple of years to work on it."

"Funny," Evelyn said, glancing at me and retreating from the room.

"When this case I'm working on is over, I'll introduce you to the Widow Plaut," I said.

"A deal," Lou said, standing and shaking my hand. For an old man, he had a strong piano-player's grip.

Lillian was no longer at the table or even in the bar when I went back into the Mozambique Lounge. There were a few more customers, all sailors. Lester was talking to the two old guys in overalls. I waved to him and he called, "Don't come back soon."

It was nice to be wanted. My next stop was Huntington Beach, where my welcome might be even less enthusiastic than this one.

I stopped for gas and two grilled-cheese sandwiches at a truck stop outside of Long Beach. The notebook in my pocket was full of charges for Fred Astaire, some of which I was having trouble reading. Less than half an hour later I was at the front door of Arthur Forbes's house, the derricks on the beach beating out like drums behind me down at the shore. There were two cars in the driveway, a black Buick and an even bigger and blacker Lincoln.

I rang. No answer. I knocked. No answer. I kept at it. I knew Carlotta Forbes was home. That is, unless she knew that her husband was dead and she was already in Los Angeles looking at the corpse and chatting with Cawelti.

The door opened. Kudlap Singh stood before and above me.

"Why aren't you with Forbes?" I asked.

"Mr. Forbes is dead," he said. "As you probably very well know."

"I thought you were his bodyguard," I said, shouting over the derricks.

"The past tense is correct. I *was* his bodyguard."

"And?"

"And," Singh went on. "This morning he told me he had an important meeting with you and Mr. Astaire. He sent me to find Mrs. Forbes. When I found her, we returned. The police were there with Mr. Forbes's body. They informed us that you and Mr. Astaire had been taken away by their captain. Mrs. Forbes asked me to bring her home immediately. I did so."

"Sort of ends a good job," I said.

"Mrs. Forbes has indicated that she wishes to retain my services."

"Congratulations," I said. "Can I talk to the grieving widow?"

"I very much doubt it," he said.

"Tell her I'm going to go talk to her father if she won't talk to me."

"I doubt if Mr. Cortona would welcome a call from you at this time," said Singh.

I stood with my hands folded in front of me.

"I'll see if Mrs. Forbes will talk to you," Singh said, closing the door.

I listened to the derricks and thought I even heard the surf. I waited. Singh opened the door and stepped out of the way. I went in. He led me to the same room I had been in with Jeremy the night before. The first thing I saw was myself in the mirrored wall. Then I saw the grieving widow properly dressed in black with a veil. I also saw three men in dark suits. Two of the men were standing. The oldest man sat in a chair. He had an ebony cane in his hand and his white hair was worn in a wave. I recognized him. He was Guiseppi Cortona. His picture had been in the papers and the *Police Gazette*. Guiseppi Cortona was the crime boss of Minneapolis. He was supposedly meaner than his former son-in-law, Fingers Intaglia. Guiseppi was reputed to cut off appendages even more valuable and vulnerable than one's fingers.

"You wanted to see me?" Cortona said.

"I was bluffing," I said.

The widow pulled back her veil and took out a cigarette. One of the men in suits moved quickly to light it for her.

"Bluffing," Cortona repeated as if the word were particularly interesting. "Bluffing about what?"

"I had some questions for Mrs. Forbes. I was afraid she wouldn't answer them."

"We were on our way back to Los Angeles to arrange for my son-in-law's funeral and talk to the authorities," Cortona said. "We were also going to look you up. A friend in the police department says you killed Arthur, you and the dancer."

"I didn't kill him," I said.

"And the two-bit, what was his name?"

"Talbott, Willie Talbott," Carlotta supplied.

"Willie Talbott. You didn't kill him either. Or the blonde . . ."

"Luna Martin," Carlotta supplied impatiently. "Papa, he killed Arthur."

"Why would I kill Arthur?"

"To get him off your client. Because he threatened to kill you. How do I know?" Carlotta said, looking around now for an ashtray for the cigarette she had barely touched. One of the two men in suits came up with one for her.

"I can't dance," said Cortona sadly, touching his leg. "Been like this since I was a kid. Truck got me in an alley in Palermo. Driver was a kid like me, doing a job. Only, he didn't come out of the alley." Cortona nodded at the two men in suits, who moved toward me as I backed up.

"I just have three questions," I said, remembering that my .38 was on the desk of John Cawelti.

"What?" asked Carlotta.

The two guys in suits were coming on. They were both bigger than they had looked across the room.

"Who introduced Luna to your husband?"

"How should I know?"

"Two more questions and then . . ." Cortona said.

"The black Buick in the driveway. That yours?"

"Yes," she said.

"Last question," said Cortona.

"What do you do with your old purses?"

"My old . . ."

"You throw them away?" I asked.

"That's four questions," Cortona said. "You're over the limit and you're asking stupid questions."

"I keep my old purses. I don't throw things away. I'm a pack rat," Carlotta said. "I hold onto my memories. And I'll hold onto the memory of what's gonna happen to you right now."

"No more questions," said Cortona, thumping his cane on the wooden floor.

I reached back for the door.

"I didn't kill him," I said.

"Then," said Cortona with a shrug, "I'm making a mistake. I have made them in the past."

I looked at Carlotta. Her veil was back down.

"An accident," Cortona said. "You got an ocean. You got oil things. Lots of places for an accident."

They took my arms and turned me out of the room.

"Not too long," Cortona called. "We've got to get to town."

"I didn't do it," I said to the two guys who walked me down the hallway and out the front door.

"We don't care," said the taller, heavier one on my right arm.

"Not in the least," said the other one.

Both were dark. Both were strong. We were on the way down the front steps. Kudlap Singh, the Beast of Bombay, was at the bottom of the steps, directly in our path.

"We're going for a walk with our friend," the bigger guy on my right said.

"He is not your friend," said Singh.

"We're still going for a walk," said the bigger guy.

"Peters is a friend to a friend of mine," said Singh.

"That is interesting," said the big guy, looking at his watch. "We're in a hurry."

"I think you should allow him to get in his car and drive away," Singh said, barring the path.

The guy on my left arm let go and reached under his open jacket. Singh stepped forward and grabbed his wrist. The guy's hand came out clutching a gun. The other guy let me go and went for his gun. I gave him a solid punch to the neck, usually effective and it didn't hurt your knuckles. Both of Guiseppi Cortona's men were on the ground. The one Singh had grabbed was clutching a broken wrist. His gun was nowhere in sight. The other guy was on his knees, gasping like an asthmatic.

"Go," Singh said to me.

"Come on," I said.

"I have a vehicle," he said. "I will find other work. Perhaps the war will end soon and I'll be able to return to India."

The one I had punched was trying to stand. His hands were around his neck. It looked as if he were trying to strangle himself.

"Thanks," I said.

I ran to my Crosley, got in, started it, and almost caught

the bumper of the Lincoln as I made it through a narrow space between car and house. In the rearview mirror, I saw the two bad guys trying to pull themselves together. Guiseppi wasn't going to be happy with them. They would have been better off coming with me.

Singh stood waiting till I was down the driveway and just about to hit the road. Then he turned slowly and walked around toward the rear of the house.

I found a turnoff about half a mile down the road, pulled in, parked where I wouldn't be seen by anyone driving by, and waited. The wait was short, about two minutes. Kudlap Singh drove past in a blue coupe. He was definitely breaking the speed limit. About five minutes later, the Lincoln zipped by in a big hurry, but I got a glimpse of the guy I had hit in the neck. He was driving. The one with the broken wrist was next to him in the passenger seat, and I saw or imagined I saw Carlotta and her old man in the back.

I drove back to the Forbes house, my heart pounding in time to the oil derricks. The front door wasn't locked. They had left in a rush, though I was sure Cortona had made at least one phone call before they piled into the Lincoln.

I found a phone on the second floor in what looked like the master bedroom: big, blue-and-white wallpaper, a bed with a dark wooden headboard the size of Rhode Island. I made two calls and started my search. It took me fifteen minutes and four rooms, but I found what I was looking for.

Forbes had said his wife was a pack rat, that she didn't throw anything away, not a grudge, not an old dress. He was right.

I headed for my car.

I knew a few more things than I knew before I had made the trip.

The most important thing I had learned was who had killed Arthur Forbes. At least I thought I knew. I was more sure of something else. Fred Astaire's life was in danger.

Chapter Thirteen

Dancing at the Moving Picture Ball

I pushed the Crosley, but there was no way I could get more than forty-five miles an hour out of it. I made one quick stop for gas, a Whiz bar, and an apple. I listened to Elmer Davis on the radio and tried to come up with more of a plan than I had. No use.

Davis reminded his listeners that the United States was an awesome power. We had put together an army of twelve million men and we were fighting two powerful empires at the same time. We had a navy bigger than the combined fleets of our enemies and allies. And we were still able to record a twenty-percent increase in annual civilian spending. Davis closed by saying that, "To America, war is a business, not an art."

It was almost dark when I got back to L.A. and pulled into a parking spot on Wilshire between a fire hydrant and a Rolls-Royce. The street was packed and the lights were bright at the Wiltern Theater. When darkness hit so would the curfew, but there were still a few minutes. I ducked traffic and ran across the street to the front of the theater, where my brother Phil and Steve Seidman stood waiting.

"You're late," Phil said, checking his watch.

"Did they start?" I asked.

"I got the schedule," said Seidman. "Ritz Brothers open, followed by Jane Withers and Allan Jones. Then Fred Astaire and Rita Hayworth. Show closes with Alice Faye and Phil Harris."

"You see Guiseppi Cortona and his daughter go in?" I asked.

"Who knows?" Phil said. "This better be something, Tobias."

"They're in there. Forbes told me he had tickets. Let's go," I said, heading for the lobby door.

"This is bullshit," Phil said, holding his ground.

"We've got no time for this," I said, "but here."

I took out what I had found hidden at the Forbes house and handed it to Phil. I showed him where he should look.

"Carlotta Forbes took dancing lessons at On Your Toes Dance Studio. Her teacher was Luna Martin. They had lots of lessons. Look."

I flipped the pages of Willie Talbott's book and showed him.

"And?"

"And," I said, looking at the lobby and hearing the laughter inside the theater, "I'd have to say Carlotta introduced Luna to her husband or got Luna to introduce herself."

"Why?" asked Phil.

"Blackmail. I'd say Carlotta was in bed with Willie and maybe even with Luna," I said.

Phil shook his head. He had heard it all before and seen it all. He was an L.A. cop.

"That's life," I said.

"So," said Phil, "Carlotta murders Luna. Carlotta goes for Willie Talbott's book to keep us from finding her connection to the dead woman. She kills Willie. No more blackmailers. Then . . ."

A couple in full evening dress hurried in late.

"Forbes finds out, maybe finds the book and has it out with Carlotta, tells her, father or no father, he's getting rid of her. Or maybe he threatens her with telling Guiseppi. He calls me and Astaire and tells us he wants to talk to us," I said. "By the time we get there, Carlotta puts a knife in her husband's heart, gets the book back if she ever lost it, calls the cops to catch me and Astaire with the body."

More laughter and applause inside the theater.

"Stupid," Phil said, running his hand over his bristly gray hair. "Why does she want to kill Fred Astaire?"

"Astaire and I went to Willie's to get the book. She's afraid Willie showed it to us before he went for the roof where she was waiting for him and she turned over the room and couldn't find the book. Carlotta knew our Willie and his room pretty well, but . . ."

"No," said Phil.

"I found the book in Carlotta's closet," I said. "The killer took it from Willie Talbott. Give me that much."

Phil and Steve Seidman exchanged looks. Steve closed his eyes and shrugged. We started moving toward the lobby. Posters announcing the "Night of Stars for Victory" were propped up all around.

A pair of men in suits and ties stopped us at the inner door. One of them asked for tickets. Phil showed his badge. The men took turns looking at it and couldn't make up their minds what to do. Phil made up their minds for them. He pocketed shield and wallet and bulled past the men, one of whom said, "Wait just a goddamn minute."

But we didn't wait. We opened the inner doors and went in.

The theater was packed and in a good mood. Jane Withers was on stage with Allan Jones. Harry Ritz was peeking, goggle-eyed, around the curtain on the right of the stage.

Every time Withers or Jones looked toward the curtain, Ritz disappeared. The audience went wild.

Cortona was in about the fourteenth row on the right. He was easy to find. There was an empty seat next to him and he was the only one not laughing at Harry Ritz. Seidman and Phil moved to the exit door on the left and went through. I excused my way into the seat next to Cortona, stepping on the foot of Edith Head. Cortona glanced at me but didn't seem surprised to see me.

"Sorry I'm late," I said.

Cortona didn't answer.

"This Carlotta's seat?"

Cortona was silent.

The audience roared as all three of the Ritz Brothers high-stepped across the stage behind Withers and Jones, who finally caught them.

"Where's Carlotta?"

Cortona closed his eyes, his chin sagged on the head of the cane held between his legs.

"I warned Arthur when he married her," he said. "She's my daughter but she's not right in the head."

I had to lean over to hear him over the laughter in the audience and the banter on stage.

"She's my only child," Cortona said, his eyes still closed. "But she's . . . she has a streak in her. A temper. I don't know where she gets it."

I had some ideas, but this wasn't the place to bring them out.

"Will you please be quiet?" a man in the row behind us said, leaning forward.

"She wanted me dead," I whispered to the old man. "And she wants Astaire dead."

He didn't answer.

"Why?" I asked.

"The book," he said. "She's afraid you saw the book. Carlotta and that Luna Martin were . . . And she blames you and Astaire for working Luna up."

"She'll be caught before . . ." I said.

"She doesn't care," he said, shaking his head. "I can tell big men with guns and knives what to do and they do it. But with her . . ."

The applause suddenly boomed and Jane Withers did a gee-whiz introduction of Astaire and Rita Hayworth. I eased my way back into the aisle and went for the door Phil and Seidman had taken.

There were two guards in brown uniforms at the stage entrance. One of them held up his hand. The other one said, "Toby, what the hell is going on? Phil just blew by and the place is going nuts."

The guard was Barry Lorie. We had both worked security at Warner Brothers. Good man, bad legs.

"Someone's trying to kill Astaire," I said.

"Shit you say."

"Straight up, Barry. You see a thin, good-looking dark woman back here, all in black?"

"Lots of 'em," said Barry. "In black, white, pink, red. You name it."

Astaire and Rita Hayworth were in the wings no more than a dozen feet from me. People were scurrying around. A guy with a clipboard was looking at his watch and doing a countdown. Astaire was in a tux and a toupee. Hayworth was in something black and frilly, her red hair billowed soft.

"Fred," I called in a loud whisper.

"Keep it down, Toby," Barry said.

I looked for Phil and Steve and couldn't find them.

Astaire turned when I called again. He saw me and said, "Toby?"

Rita Hayworth turned toward me, teeth white, lips red, puzzled. The orchestra began to play "Lovely to Look At."

"Carlotta Forbes did it," I said. "She's here tonight. She's after . . ." but Astaire couldn't hear me over the music.

"Now," said the guy with the clipboard.

And Hayworth and Astaire flowed onto the stage to wild applause.

"Barry?" I asked.

He nodded and let me pass.

I pushed my way through dancers, comics, and novelty acts, all waiting, all trying to be quiet. No Carlotta. I looked onto the stage where Astaire and Hayworth seemed to float about an inch off the floor. And then I saw her. Carlotta was in the wings on the other side of the stage. She had a big purse in her hand and her hand in the purse.

"I've got to get to the other side," I whispered to an old guy in a cap who was working on the rigging. "Fast."

"Flat goes clear to the back wall," he said. "Either go out and around, or you go right across the stage. Lots of people out there."

Carlotta's hand was slowly coming out of her purse. I was pretty sure of what was in that hand. I looked around for Phil. Nothing.

I tore off my jacket and tapped the shoulder of a curly-haired guy just about my size. He was whispering to a pretty blonde in a big purple-and-white turban. The guy turned to me. It was Cornel Wilde.

"I need your jacket," I said.

"My . . ."

"Police," I said, pointing to my empty holster. "Hurry."

Wilde looked at the blonde and then turned to me, taking off his jacket.

"Anything I can do to help?" he asked.

"Pray," I said, putting on the jacket and taking the hand of the blonde girl.

"Wait," she squealed as I pulled her toward the stage.

"We're gonna dance across that stage," I said. "We're gonna save Fred Astaire's life."

The blonde turned to Wilde, who said, "Do it."

I pushed past the guy with the clipboard, took a deep breath, and danced the blonde out onto the stage, doing my best to imagine I was Fred Astaire.

There was a rumble of confused conversation in the audience.

Astaire and Hayworth swirled around and Astaire gave me a questioning look. I nodded toward the far wing and he turned his eyes toward Carlotta, who was definitely taking something out of her purse. I kept dancing. The look on Carlotta's face might have said a lot of things. I thought it said, "This is my lucky night. I've got them both out there."

But it was hard to imagine what Carlotta was thinking. She was about to murder a movie star on stage, in front of a few thousand people, to cover up another murder. There was no chance of her getting away with this. And then I realized what she was doing. It was her relationship to Luna Martin she was covering. She didn't care if she was dragged away in cuffs as long as no one could suggest a relationship to Luna.

I turned, more or less to the music, and the blonde beamed at the audience and guided me through the couple of dozen feet across the stage.

"Light and lead me," she whispered like a ventriloquist through clenched teeth.

I nodded and looked at her.

I was dancing with Betty Grable.

We had almost made it across the stage when Carlotta, her back to the people in the wing, came out with the gun. Almost, but not quite. I wasn't going to get to her in time. My best bet was to get Astaire and Hayworth down and hope Carlotta missed. I danced toward them and was about to throw myself onto Astaire and Hayworth when I heard a scuffling over the music and saw my brother grab Carlotta's wrist, pull the gun from her hand, and pull her back into the shadows.

I was in the middle of the stage now, with Betty Grable in my arms. The lights were in my eyes but I could feel the people out there. Suddenly, somehow, Astaire and Hayworth orchestrated a partner-change and I found Rita Hayworth in my arms. She smelled like the few good memories of my battered life.

The audience went wild with applause. Astaire and Betty Grable went twirling past us.

"You'd better have a goddamn good explanation for this," Hayworth said with an enormous smile. "And don't step on my toes."

I don't know what I did for the next minute or so. I know I didn't step on Rita Hayworth's toes. Then, mercifully, the music stopped. She led me to the front of the stage. Astaire and Grable were there. We all joined hands and bowed. The audience went wild.

The lights were coming up as the curtain slowly lowered in front of us. I looked for Guiseppi Cortona. His seat was empty.

"Explain," said Rita Hayworth, her hands on her hips when the curtain was all the way down.

The crowd was still applauding wildly and asking for more.

"Toby is more or less my bodyguard," Astaire explained. "I think he just saved my life."

Betty Grable took my hand and said, "I've got to get ready

for my number. I don't know what this was all about, but I think it was fun."

And she was gone.

"Mr. Astaire, Miss Hayworth, please clear the stage for the next number," the guy with the clipboard said, looking at me.

We moved off stage and as I passed Cornel Wilde I handed him his jacket. He patted my shoulder and moved onto the stage.

"Rita," Astaire said, taking one of her hands in both of his, "trust me."

She looked at me, shook her head, and said, "Well, it was an experience I haven't had before."

And she was gone.

The orchestra had already started its next number.

"Best dancer I've ever worked with," Astaire said, hands in his pockets as we watched her move away through the backstage crowd. And then he turned to me: "Toby, is it over?"

"Almost," I said. "I've got to go. I'll send you a bill."

"You were pretty good out there," he said.

"I had a great teacher," I answered and moved past Barry Lorie and the other guard.

I went through the stage-door exit, down an alley, and back to Wilshire. I didn't want to run into Phil. He'd want me to give a statement and help make sense out of what Carlotta might be telling him.

If he got her talking, there was one big piece of the puzzle she couldn't help him with. Carlotta had murdered Willie Talbott and her husband, but she hadn't killed Luna Martin.

I was hungry. I was tired. I had just danced with Betty Grable and Rita Hayworth on the stage of the Wiltern Theater and I was on my way to do something I didn't want to do.

Chapter Fourteen

After the Ball Was Over

"You look rotten," Lester Gannett said when I leaned against the bar of the Mozambique.

There wasn't much of a crowd, maybe fifteen, twenty people, and Evelyn the chanteuse was not holding them in the palm of her gloved hand with her version of "Lili Marlene."

"It's been a long few days," I said.

"Make that a lifetime," said a fat woman on the stool next to me.

"I thought you were never gonna come back here," Lester said. "We had an agreement."

"I'll make it quick," I said.

"You still look rotten. You need a shave and a bath."

"He's not the only one," the fat woman said.

Evelyn belted and Lou rippled the keys behind her.

"I've been dancing with Betty Grable and Rita Hayworth," I explained.

"Right," said Lester. "And I've got Gene Tierney waitin' for me upstairs. Toby, make it fast and get the hell out of here."

Sidney the cockatoo let out a shriek, upstaging Evelyn. Then Sidney said, "Phooey on the Fuhrer."

"Amen to that," said the fat lady, holding up her glass.

I made my way to a booth and sat in the shadows till the set was over. There was a round of applause to which Evelyn and her pink boa responded with a bow. There was no second round. When she had left the stage and Lou had announced that he would be back in a few minutes to play favorites, I got up and followed him.

Going across the platform of the Mozambique was not like playing the Wiltern.

As soon as I got through the door, I could hear Evelyn shouting, "You were off. You were off half a goddamn beat the whole set. Where's your mind, you old fart. This is my career here."

I found them in Lou's dressing room/home. He was sitting at his mirror. She was still going.

"I gotta take hold here," she said, lowering her voice a little but not much. "I'm down to playin' toilets like this with a piano player who . . . oh, shit. Forget it."

She turned, saw me, pushed past, and slammed the door.

"Lady's upset," I said, sitting on the edge of the bed.

"Lady can't carry a tune," Lou answered. "When she talks the song through, she is somewhere between terrible and dreck. When she sings, she can drive a musician to suicide."

"I heard that," Evelyn said, bursting back into the room.

"Listening at the door," Lou said, looking at me. "No privacy. No respect."

"I'm gonna have your ass."

"Good," said Lou. "No one's wanted it for thirty years."

"I'm gonna get you canned," Evelyn said, advancing on Lou, who stood up.

"Leave," he said softly. "This is what I have left of a home. I don't want the shrill and untalented intruding."

"I'll . . ." she started.

Lou took her arm in his thin hand and turned her around

toward the door. She tried to pull loose but couldn't do it. Lou opened the door. Evelyn began to cry.

"This is not fair," she sobbed.

"What you need is another line of work," said Lou, ushering her out and closing the door behind her.

"You've got strong hands," I said.

Lou looked at his hands.

"I play piano. Seventy years I play piano. Of course I've got strong hands." He turned his chair and sat to face me. "So," he said. "First you give me financial security and now you come to me with bad news, right?"

"Right," I said.

"You know?" he answered.

"I know," I answered.

"Tell me, so I know we're talking about the same thing," he said.

"You killed Luna Martin."

"We're talking about the same thing."

"You were in the hall," I said. "She couldn't have gone more than a few feet when she died. You had to see who did it. They had to do it while you were standing there."

"How did I do it, Philo Vance? I didn't have a knife."

"Piano wire," I said. "There was a bad note on the piano. You were working on it, went out, probably to get a new wire from a piano somewhere else in the hotel. Who knows. You met Luna in the hall. You killed her. You took the wire and put it in your pocket. She staggered in, pointed to the piano, and dropped dead. Unfortunately for Shelly Minck, he was standing between Luna and the piano when she pointed."

Lou smiled, shook his head, and touched his mustache. He looked a lot older than eighty.

"You know how I got away with it?" he asked. "I'm an old man. Nobody pays attention to an old man. Nobody would even consider that an old man could kill a big young woman. I was invisible. The police barely talked to me. I was just a crotchety old fart who was losing his memory."

"Why, Lou?"

"Nothing fancy," Lou said with a sigh, looking around his small room. "She insulted me, ridiculed me, like Evelyn, only worse. You heard her. She was even worse in the hall, and she caught me at a bad time. My liver's going. My heart is bad. All I've got is my memories and a bagful of old songs. She said I had ruined her lesson, called me an old sack of shit, said I should have died long ago. I told her I had played for Nora Bayes, Sophie Tucker, played with the best in Orleans, the best, colored and white both. She laughed and turned her back. I had the wire."

Lou shrugged again.

"I guess this means I won't be meeting the mysterious Mrs. Platt."

"Plaut," I said.

"You think they've got pianos in prison?" he asked. "Hell, I'm gonna die soon anyway. I'd die faster without a piano, you know what I'm saying?"

"I know, Lou," I said getting up. "I'll get back to you."

"Life is a surprise," he said.

"I've noticed," I said.

An hour later I was on my way up the steps inside Mrs. Plaut's boardinghouse. It was two in the morning and my shoes were off. I made it to my room. There was no one there but Dash, who was sitting on the ledge of the open window, looking up at the moon. He turned to look at me for an instant and then turned back to the moon.

I got undressed and made myself a bowl of Wheaties with milk. I did the same for Dash, who tore himself away from the nightlife to join me at the table.

When we were finished, I scratched Dash's head for a

minute or two and then turned out the lights and got down on my mattress. Moonlight lit the room gently, and Dash curled up next to me, purring.

I was asleep before I could review the day and worry about tomorrow.

Chapter Fifteen

Save the Last Dance for Me

"The dawn has broken," came the voice of Mrs. Plaut, waking me from a dream of dancing on a cloud with Anita Maloney.

Anita was wearing her prom dress and a big white corsage. The cloud was in the middle of the Glendale High gym. Anita was sixteen and I was eighteen.

"The dawn has broken," Mrs. Plaut repeated.

Anita and I began to sink into the cloud.

I opened my eyes. Mrs. Plaut stood over me in a blue dress and an apron. She was carrying a feather duster.

"Thanks for the information," I said, checking to see if she was wearing her hearing aid. She wasn't.

"Where?" she asked.

"Where what?" I shouted.

She looked at me as if I were feebleminded and said, "You have a call."

She turned and left the room. The Beech-Nut Gum clock said it was a little before seven. I got up, slipped on the pants I had thrown on the chair the night before, and went into the hall to get the phone.

"Hello," I said.

"She confessed," Phil said. "Killed Talbott and Forbes,

said they were blackmailing her. Said she got her father to try to scare you off. She says she, Luna, and Talbott were planning to get rid of Forbes. Carlotta was a busy lady. She was having affairs with Luna Martin and Willie Talbott. She claims she didn't kill Luna. She loved her. Steve and I have been up all night with her."

"You think she killed Luna?"

"Who else?" Phil asked. "Goddamn perverted city. Women making love to women. Men making love to men. If any of my kids . . ."

"Get some sleep, Phil."

"Yeah," he said. "Cawelti wants to see you. He's mad as hell that Steve and I broke the case. He said if you want your gun back and you want to keep your license, you be in his office before ten."

"I'll be there."

"You did a good job, Tobias," he said.

He hung up. It was the best conversation I had ever had with my brother.

I shaved, showered, got dressed, and tiptoed past Mrs. Plaut's door. This morning I wasn't so lucky. She came out of her door and blocked my path.

"You mentioned yesterday, I believe, that you knew a possible gentleman caller."

"I did," I confessed.

"Give him this and tell him I will be receiving in my parlor on Saturday next between noon and four. There will be tea and sweets."

"I'll tell him," I said loudly, taking the package.

"Meyerpresent cakes," she said, pointing at the package.

"Smells good," I said, lowering my voice. "About the gentleman. You should know he's a murderer."

"That is fine," she said. "The Mister was a Methodist."

Ten minutes later I was having a pair of tacos and a cup of

coffee at Manny's. Manny told me the war news and I kept an eye out for Juanita. If she came, I planned to retreat through the back door. She didn't come.

Shelly was in the office, humming away. Violet hadn't yet arrived.

"Mildred welcome you back?" I asked.

"With conditions," he said, turning to me as he set up his instruments for his first victim of the day. "I've got to take her to Mexico for a vacation and I've got to fire Violet."

"And you're going to fire Violet?"

"No," he said. "You are. We're partners."

"We are?"

"Always have been," he said. "We share an office, a receptionist. You call on me when you need a hand. I call on you."

"We are not partners, Shel. You want to fire Violet, do it yourself."

"Concessions," he said, turning to me and removing his morning cigar from his mouth. "Two months' rent on the sublet free. You fire her."

"Tell Mildred Violet works for me. I'll pay her."

"But Mildred . . ."

"Forget it, Shel. I pay her. She works for me."

I headed for my cubbyhole office with the package of Meyerpresent cakes for Lou Canton. Hell, I wouldn't be seeing Lou till next Saturday. I knew I'd be picking him up to call on Mrs. Plaut. The package smelled great. I got behind my desk and opened the box. There were four round cakes. I started to eat one while I pulled out a sheet of paper and started preparing my bill for Fred Astaire.

Shelly burst in. "Maybe we can work something out," he said frantically. "I tell Mildred Violet works for you and she'll have to talk to you about firing her. I cut four dollars a month from your rent and you tell Violet to keep doing what she's been doing for me."

"No more rent on this closet, Shel, and I pay Violet. Best offer. Take it or leave it. You want a Meyerpresent cake?"

He took one, removed the cigar from his mouth, adjusted his glasses, and took a gigantic bite. That left two cakes for Lou. I knew I'd eat them. They were great and they'd be hard as coconuts by Saturday.

"All right," Shelly said, taking the remains of his cake and leaving.

There were four notes on my desk, all in Violet's neat hand. Before I looked at them, I typed up my bill for Fred Astaire:

Bill for Investigative Services:
Basic retainer (three days) *$75.00*
Accompanist (Lou Canton) for dance lessons *$50.00*
Parking (Monticello Hotel parking lot) *$7.00*
Actors (Pook Hurawitz, Jerry Rogasinian) *$40.00*
Cab fare for accompanist *$4.00*
Poplin jacket (torn during pursuit of killer) *$5.40*
For information from desk clerk at Monticello *$10.00*
Parking ticket *$3.00*
Gas to Huntington Beach (two round trips) *$5.00*
Total *$199.40*

Astaire had given me a $200.00 advance. I subtracted my own fee ($75.00) which left $125.00. The total expenses listed came to $134.40, which meant that Fred Astaire owed me $9.40. I looked at the finished bill and tore it up. I still had what was left of the five hundred bucks one of Cortona's men had left on the front seat of my car, and all of the five hundred Forbes had given me.

I looked at my phone messages.

Hy of Hy's for Him called. He had a job for me.

Jack Ellis, a house detective at one of the downtown hotels, wanted to know if I would cover for him when he went on vacation next month.

A woman named Levine called, saying, "Where's my cat?" I had searched for her missing cat more than three years ago. I had returned her fee. I had begged her to forget it, but she emerged to haunt me every four or five months.

The last message was the most interesting. It read: "Mr. Fields would like you to call him as soon as possible. A matter of great importance."

There was a phone number and a time.

My day was planned. Finish my bill to Astaire. Go see Captain Cawelti. Retrieve my .38. To Mack's Diner for lunch and Anita and an invitation for her to go out dancing Saturday night.

I hummed a few bars of "Lovely to Look At" and picked up the phone to call W.C. Fields.